CANDLELIGHT REGENCY SPECIAL

Candlelight Regencies

COMPROMISED LOVE

****

Anne Hillary

A Candlelight Regency Special

To Eric and Brian

Published by
Dell Publishing Co., Inc.
1 Dag Hammarskjold Plaza
New York, New York 10017

Dell ® TM 681510, Dell Publishing Co., Inc.

ISBN: 0–440–11351–2

Printed in the United States of America

First printing—June 1981

COMPROMISED
LOVE

CHAPTER ONE

Two stablehands came across the courtyard, the stable door swinging closed behind them. One was carrying a heavy saddle that needed polishing; the other was loaded down with bridles and harnesses to be repaired. They were talking together loudly and did not notice the two young people hiding behind the hedge.

Once the men had disappeared into their workroom, the girl rushed forward. She was small and wore a mud-spattered riding habit. Although its style made her look twelve years old instead of seventeen, a discerning eye could see womanly curves beneath its childish lines.

Her reddish-brown hair was pulled back, but loose

curls fell freely around her face. She wore deep brown riding gloves that looked conspicuously new amid her untidiness. At the moment, though, she was more concerned with persuading her companion to come out of his hiding place than with her appearance.

"Oh, do come out, Laurie," she pleaded. "Now's our chance."

Lawrence Kendall came out of the bushes reluctantly. He was only a year older than the girl, but almost a foot taller. He was dressed in dark green broadcloth and buckskin. His white shirt was immaculate, and his dark brown hair was neat, despite a strong breeze.

"I don't think we ought to," he protested weakly. "Anthony would never forgive me. He's waited so long for Moonlight to foal, and now that she has, he's terribly protective about the colt."

The girl stopped and put her hands on her hips. "Oh, pooh!" she said, stamping her foot in frustration. "Anthony will never know. We're only going in for a moment." She smiled coaxingly. "Besides, it's my birthday, so you have to do what I want."

"That's not fair, Stacy," Laurie pointed out. "I already gave you a present."

Stacy relented immediately. "I know, and I do love them. I never had a pair of such nice riding gloves." She came over, put her arm through his, and looked up at him contritely. Laurie blushed as she moved close to him, watching her with sudden wariness, but Stacy could sense his reluctant change of mind.

"There's nothing else to do, since we've finished riding," she pointed out. "And I don't want to go home yet. So let's slip in and see the foal. That can be Anthony's present to me," she added with a laugh.

Laurie allowed himself to be led forward. "I didn't know that Anthony ever gave you a present," he said as she pulled open the stable door.

"He hasn't," Stacy admitted with a grin, "so don't you think he owes me one?"

The stable was dark after the bright sunlight outside, and they stood inside the doorway for a moment until they could see around them. Laurie pointed silently toward a stall at the far end, and Stacy hurried toward it. Laurie followed reluctantly, glancing nervously about.

In the large stall at the end of the stable, a pure white mare was standing guard over her foal. He was sleeping in the hay at his mother's feet, but Stacy could see that he was black with a white star on his face. Moonlight moved restlessly at the sound of Stacy's approach, and the foal sleepily opened his eyes and raised his head.

"Oh, he's beautiful, Moonlight," Stacy whispered to the mare. She knelt down on the stable floor and peered through the bars that closed off the stall. The foal had gone back to sleep. "You must be very proud of him," Stacy told Moonlight as the big horse moved closer to her. She reached down and snorted her hot breath into Stacy's hand.

"Let's go," Laurie pleaded nervously.

"Always begging for food, aren't you?" Stacy laughed at the horse. She reached into her pocket and pulled out a carrot. Moonlight took it from her hand, her large white teeth carefully avoiding Stacy's skin. She crunched it noisily and snorted for more.

"That's all, you greedy little beggar," Stacy laughed, rubbing the horse's nose. "It was your garden that I raided, so I had to be quick."

When Moonlight realized that there was no more food, she moved back over to the foal. Stacy took a last look, then stood up with a sigh. She turned toward Laurie, and saw, with a start, someone move at the other end of the stable.

"What are you two doing in here?" a cold voice demanded.

They stood still, staring into the shadows as Anthony, Laurie's older brother, moved closer to them. He had the same dark hair and eyes as Laurie, and was dressed with the same meticulous care, but the resemblance ended there. Besides being taller and more muscular than Laurie, there was a stern, unapproachable air about him. He ran his estate with grim efficiency, guided by his idea of duty and social convention. He was always totally in control of himself and of any situation he was in, but he seemed to take no pleasure in that fact.

"I thought I gave explicit instructions that no one was to come in here and disturb my horses," he said, looking at Laurie.

Stacy glanced quickly at Laurie and saw that he was cowering in the face of his brother's displeasure. She stepped forward quickly, angry that her friend should be humiliated.

"I wanted to see the foal," she said defiantly, moving between Laurie and his brother.

Anthony's eyebrows raised slightly at her action, but Stacy refused to be intimidated. Anthony had no feelings, she knew, but Laurie did, and she was not about to let his heartless brother trample them into the dust.

"I don't care what you want," Anthony told her. "This foal is not as strong as he should be, and I don't want him disturbed."

"Oh, but we did not disturb any of your horses," Stacy pointed out politely. "We were ever so quiet." She looked about her as some of the horses moved restlessly. "I do think, though, that they sense your anger, and that can't be good for them." She smiled sweetly at him, while Laurie sucked in his breath in horror. No one talked to Anthony like that!

Anthony's eyes flashed angrily, and his lips tightened to a thin, ominous line, but Stacy stood her ground. She was determined not to tremble in fear,

11

as Laurie did. After a tense moment of silence Anthony spoke again. "Will you please leave?" It was a command, not a request.

"Why certainly," Stacy agreed. "We were just going when you stopped us." She might have said more, but Laurie had grabbed her arm and was dragging her toward the door. Just as they reached it, she turned back to Anthony. "It's a beautiful foal," she called out to him with a smile. She waved cheerfully as Laurie pulled her through the door.

"Why must you always rile him so?" Laurie asked in despair as the stable door closed behind him. "He was furious with you."

"Was he?" Stacy shrugged unconcernedly. "He's so remote, it's hard to tell." She looked at Laurie, who was still glancing nervously at the door. "It will do him good to see that some people are not afraid of him." Laurie blushed, but Stacy went on. "You'd think that he was going to eat you, the way you rush so to please him."

"He's a very good brother," Laurie said defensively.

Stacy gave him a disgusted look and walked across the courtyard to the edge of the orchard. She threw herself down on the grass, lying on her stomach, and picked at the wildflowers that grew there.

Laurie lowered himself down next to her. He watched her cautiously, trying to judge her mood. Stacy had always been the best of companions, but just lately he had noticed that she had become moody and restless. The strangest things would throw her into a fit of despondency or a terrible temper. The latter was her reaction whenever he mentioned Anthony's name.

This was hard for Laurie to understand, for he greatly admired his older brother. During a sickly childhood spent at home with tutors, Anthony had been the one who always had time for him. Their father had died when Laurie was six, and their mother had been an invalid, weakened from a series of miscarriages and stillbirths in the years after Anthony was born. Although Laurie's birth had debilitated her even further, she managed to hang on for eight years, guarding his health zealously.

Anthony was eighteen when he became Laurie's guardian, and he tried hard to give him a more normal childhood. It was difficult at first, for the years of pampering were hard to erase, and Laurie had become far too timid. Anthony brought in skilled tutors, for Laurie was too illness-prone to be sent away to school. Anthony took him about the estate and encouraged him to ride. Laurie meekly acceded to all of Anthony's wishes but did not enjoy any of it.

It wasn't until a scruffy little girl from the next estate laughed at Laurie for falling off his horse that he really tried to improve. Soon she wasn't laughing at him anymore but was challenging him to races and showing him the secret places she had discovered in the neighboring countryside.

By the time Anthony learned about Stacy, she and Laurie were fast friends. He had noticed a change in Laurie's attitude. He did seem more interested in the world about him, but Anthony never considered that that might be due to Stacy's influence, not his. To Anthony, Stacy's only value was to provide the youthful companionship that all children needed.

Stacy's and Laurie's friendship benefited both of them. Stacy's parents had died when she was only an infant, leaving her in the care of a London lawyer, for she had no relatives. She lived alone in a big house with her servants and a governess for companionship. She was never farther from home than the local village where she attended church each Sunday. She met other girls there but quickly tired of their talk of fashions and their giggling references to boys.

Stacy had two loves in her life—her books and riding, interests that Laurie shared with her. It helped to form a bond that grew stronger and stronger as time passed. Stacy's happiest moments were spent riding around the Hertfordshire countryside, where she would tease Laurie and dare him to attempt outrageous feats, while he would laughingly try to keep up with her.

Stacy never tried to pamper or protect him from risks. She would laugh at him if he tried to resort to his former timidity, but she knew how fragile his self-confidence was. If anyone ever threatened that, she recklessly threw herself to Laurie's defense, and it seemed to her that it was usually from Anthony that these attacks came.

As they sat on the grass in the orchard, Laurie looked at Stacy's hunched shoulders with a sudden rush of affection. He doubted that there was anyone besides himself who truly cared what happened to her. As he watched, she reached for a flower far from her, and her jacket was molded tightly to her body, showing the soft curve of her breast. With a start Laurie realized that she wasn't a child any longer. He felt a surprising need to take care of her and protect her. She turned to look at him, and he blushed a fiery red, fearing that she could read his thoughts.

"What is Anthony going to name the foal? Do you know?" she asked, giving him a puzzled look.

"Maybe he'll let Blanche name it," Laurie said, nervously avoiding her eyes. "After all, he is going to marry her."

Stacy sat up with interest, forgetting Laurie's strange behavior. "Don't tell me that the perfect Lord Anthony Kendall has actually fallen in love!" she cried in amazement.

Laurie shook his head, laughing at her look of astonishment. "I don't think so," he said. "Blanche is a trifle"—he paused, searching for the right word—"too orderly to inspire love."

Stacy wrinkled her nose in disgust. "In other words, they are perfectly matched."

"But I don't think they are," Laurie said in a worried tone. "I know that Anthony is always very composed, but Blanche is even worse. A statue has more feeling than she does."

"Oh, Laurie, you fuss like an old mother hen. If Anthony is as clever as you say he is, then he knows exactly what she is like." She stood up, brushing the grass from her skirt. "It sounds to me like they are just right for one another. Miss Prim and Lord Proper. I can just see her now."

Stacy put her hands on her hips and frowned down at Laurie where he lay. "I thought I gave instructions that no one was to disturb my horses," she mimicked Anthony's scolding in a high-pitched voice. "You should not be in here."

Laurie had to laugh, for she had copied his brother's mannerisms perfectly.

"Excuse me," a cool voice interrupted them.

Stacy turned, her hands still on her hips, and saw Anthony not five feet away from her. The look of anger on his face made it all too clear that he had heard what she had said and was not amused.

Stacy was ashamed. Even if she did not like Anthony, it was terribly rude of her to make fun of his fiancée, whom she had never even met. Her hands fell to her sides, and she bit her lips nervously under

Anthony's scathing glare. As Laurie scrambled to his feet, she stumbled out an apology.

Anthony ignored her and turned to his brother. "If you can spare me a few minutes, I should like to speak to you." He turned and gave Stacy another cold glance. "Alone," he added. Then he turned and walked quickly back to the house.

"I had better go," Laurie mumbled.

"I understand," she nodded, trying to smile. "Tell him everything was my fault. I'm sure he believes that anyway."

"I couldn't do that." Laurie was shocked, suddenly becoming quite chivalrous. He squared his shoulders, trying to summon the courage to face his brother.

"Do what you like," she said simply, and walked over to the fence where her horse was tied. "But it was my doing, whatever you say." She nimbly climbed up onto the fence and mounted her horse. She gave Laurie a quick wave and headed her horse through the orchard toward her home.

After a hurried ride through the orchard and across the fields, Stacy raced up to her room to find her maid waiting for her.

When sixteen-year-old Mary Miller had been hired as Stacy's maid, she had seen the job as the first step in an illustrious career as a lady's maid. She had no doubt that word of her talent would spread and that she would soon have her choice of jobs with ladies of great renown. The next two years were spent fighting frustration. There was no chance for anyone to learn of her talents, for all of Mary's efforts had failed to change Stacy's untidy appearance one bit.

"Yer gonna be late fer tea," Mary moaned as she quickly pulled off Stacy's riding habit, then pushed her into a chair by the dressing table.

Mary was pulling a comb through Stacy's tangled mass of hair when they heard a carriage approaching. "Oo, why must ya always be late?" Mary scolded, and tugged even harder on the comb.

Stacy winced and tried to shake her head free of the comb. "It's only Mr. Barlowe," Stacy said. "He just wants to be sure that I'm still alive, so he can collect his fees."

Mary made a shocked sound and gave up on Stacy's hair. Exposure to the sun and the wind had made it dry and difficult to manage, so she pulled it back with a ribbon and hurried over to get the dress she had already laid out on Stacy's bed.

"You know," Stacy said as Mary pulled the white muslin dress over her head, "I'm tired of this room."

Mary stopped buttoning long enough to look about at the sparsely furnished room. There were no ruffles or frills to indicate that a young lady slept there. "And well ye might be," she agreed.

"Perhaps Mr. Barlowe will give me the money for a new coverlet," Stacy suggested.

"A coverlet!" Mary cried. "Why, ye need a whole new room, a whole new house, fer that matter!" She went back to buttoning the dress, noting how tightly the material pulled across Stacy's chest. "And a whole new wardrobe," she muttered.

Stacy shook her head with a smile, but she knew that Mary was partially right. The house and her wardrobe could stand some improvements. Her parents had lived here for only a year after inheriting it from an elderly relative. They had made the major repairs but had died before they had the chance really to decorate it. As her guardian, Mr. Barlowe made sure that the house stayed in repair and that a competent agent managed the estate, but he made no attempt to suit the furnishings to the home of a young girl.

Miss Tessland, the governess, might have tried to steer his choices toward the things that Stacy would prefer, but she firmly believed that one in service should never dare to question her superiors. Mr. Barlowe had hired her, so his every decision was correct beyond any doubt.

After gaining Mary's reluctant approval of her appearance, Stacy went down the stairs. She was looking forward to tea, for on her birthday the cook always made her favorite chocolate cake.

Stacy let herself into the drawing room and saw

with surprise that Mr. Barlowe was not her only guest. A plump, middle-aged man was sitting on a sofa across from the others. He bounced up and smiled happily as she entered.

Stacy smiled back at him uncertainly as Mr. Barlowe rushed over to greet her. "Eustacia!" he effused. "How good it is to see you!" He reached out and took her hand in greeting.

This was so far from his usual businesslike attitude that Stacy could only stare at him in surprise. He appeared not to notice her silence and led her over to the stranger's side.

"I thought another guest would make your birthday more festive for you"—he sounded anxious to please her—"so I brought Mr. Palmer with me."

Stacy smiled a greeting to Mr. Palmer and tried not to think how much she would have preferred Laurie's presence. She chided herself for being unfair to Mr. Palmer, and, trying to make her smile more welcoming, she sat down on the sofa.

Tessie and Stacy poured cups of tea and passed out slices of chocolate cake, while Mr. Barlowe made a determined effort to converse with Stacy.

"Tell me," he smiled at her, "how have you progressed with your watercolors?"

Mr. Palmer smiled hopefully, apparently ready to admire her portfolio, while Tessie looked worried.

"I haven't done much painting since your last visit," Stacy said hesitantly.

Mr. Barlowe nodded. "You've gone back to your embroidery, then." He turned to Mr. Palmer. "Eustacia shows great promise as a needlewoman. Her sampler was a work of art."

Tessie blushed at the praise, but her worried look stayed in place, for she had been so anxious for Stacy to appear accomplished in some area that she had done most of the sampler herself.

"Actually, I spend most of my time riding," Stacy admitted.

"And wishing you could join the local hunt, I'll wager," Mr. Palmer suggested knowingly.

Before Stacy could vehemently deny such a wish, Tessie was answering for her. "Oh, yes," she said, to Stacy's astonishment, "that is one of her fondest dreams. She is so anxious to take her place amid the local gentry."

"She should be highly regarded by them when she does, for she has a great many accomplishments, thanks to you," Mr. Barlowe said to Tessie, who was overcome by such high praise.

Stacy bit back a smile and turned with interest to her piece of cake. She would leave this playacting to the others, for she was more interested in her tea. She had just taken a big bite of her cake, delighting in the gooey sweetness of the icing, when Mr. Palmer leaned close to her.

"I've brought you a little gift for your birthday,"

he said quietly to her, holding out a small wrapped package.

Stacy stared at him in surprise, unable to speak with her mouth full of cake. She quickly swallowed it and wiped the smears of icing from her face. It seemed very odd to her that a stranger should bring her a gift, and she glanced across at Tessie, depending on her guidance in gracefully refusing it; but Tessie was looking on with approval, openly curious about the contents of the box.

Stacy took the gift uneasily, forcing herself to look interested. Perhaps it was just a little trinket that he had picked up because Mr. Barlowe had mentioned it was her birthday. She pulled the paper off and opened the box to reveal a brooch. It was made in the shape of a rose with gold petals and a red stone in the center. Stacy thought it was hideous, but she knew it was no cheap trinket.

"Oh, isn't it lovely?" Tessie cooed her admiration. "Why don't you try it on?"

Stacy ignored her and turned to the man at her side. "It is very pretty, Mr. Palmer," she said.

"Hugo," he interrupted with a smile. "Call me Hugo."

"All right, Hugo," she said halfheartedly. "But surely you must realize that I can't accept a gift like this from you. It would be most improper."

"But it would look so nice on you," he coaxed, not sounding ashamed for his impropriety at all.

"Do try it on," Tessie urged. Mr. Barlowe nodded in agreement.

Stacy felt cornered as she pinned the brooch to her dress with stiff fingers. Her apprehension grew as she sat, unsmiling, through the exclamations of praise.

"It was one of Dora's favorites," Mr. Palmer told them proudly.

"Dora?" Stacy asked.

"My wife," he explained. "She would have liked you to have it."

Stacy could think of no reason why his wife should want her to have one of her favorite pieces of jewelry. Mr. Barlowe quietly explained further.

"Dora died just over a year ago," he said.

"How terrible for you," Stacy sympathized. "You must miss her very much."

Mr. Palmer nodded, his smile dimming slightly. "Yes, she was an angel," he sighed, "even though she never managed to give me an heir. She was so disappointed when Octavia was born that she died."

"But you have a daughter?" Stacy ventured. "She must be some comfort to you now that your wife is gone."

Mr. Palmer looked at her strangely. "You misunderstood me," he corrected her gently. "Octavia was the eighth. Eight girls." He shook his head sadly. "And not one boy."

He stared dejectedly at the table while Stacy quickly returned to her cup of tea. She might be inexperienced in society, but she knew that this was not normal drawing-room conversation. She was quite relieved when Mr. Barlowe stood up, ready to depart.

"But we'll see you both soon," he said as they took their leave. "We are looking forward to dining with you tonight."

The two men bowed, and as they left the room Stacy sank into a chair in relief. Their presence had frightened her, for some reason she could not quite explain, and the fact that they were returning filled her with apprehension. She looked up to see Tessie smiling happily at her.

"Why did Mr. Barlowe bring Mr. Palmer here, Tessie?" she asked suspiciously. "They didn't just happen by for tea."

Tessie looked anxious, and Stacy found herself becoming tense again.

"That brooch is quite lovely," Tessie said, pouring herself a cup of cold tea.

"It may be, but he had no right to give me a gift like that," Stacy pointed out.

"Oh, I don't know," Tessie argued. "I imagine that he'll give you all of his wife's jewelry."

"Why on earth would he do that?" Stacy demanded of her. "I don't want it."

Tessie turned to stare at her in surprise, amazement plain in her pale blue eyes. "Surely you understood why he was here," she said, knowing that Stacy didn't.

Stacy jumped up, her hands clenched tightly. "That's what I'm trying to find out," she cried. "Why *was* he here?"

"Because Mr. Barlowe has arranged for you to marry him," Tessie said simply.

Stacy felt all the blood drain from her face, and she sat down in a daze. It was what she had feared, with his improper gift and Tessie's strange behavior, but she had hoped, prayed, that she was wrong.

"What makes Mr. Barlowe so sure that I will want to marry Mr. Palmer?" she asked Tessie quietly.

"There is no question of what you want," Tessie scolded her lightly. "The decision is solely up to Mr. Barlowe. He is your guardian, and you have no say in the matter at all."

"But I don't want to marry Mr. Palmer, or anybody yet," Stacy argued. "I'm only seventeen."

"Many girls of your age are married," Tessie said, refusing to argue. She had always had great faith in the lawyer's wisdom, and she could not understand why Stacy was doubting him. "Mr. Barlowe thinks you should be married. He has made the decision and has found someone kind and considerate for you. I should think you'd be excited about the prospect of such a pleasant life, rather than complaining about what you can't change."

Tessie marched from the room, holding her head

high. She closed the door solidly behind her, in spite of the anguished look she had seen on Stacy's face.

CHAPTER TWO

"You spend far too much of your time with that girl," Anthony said, looking particularly forbidding. "Her behavior is atrocious and yet you join in all her escapades. I cannot allow it any longer." He leaned back in his chair and looked at Laurie across the gleaming expanse of his desk.

"I say, Anthony," Laurie protested weakly, nervously striding closer. "I am eighteen, you know. I'm not a child that you can order about."

"Then it's time you were more responsible in your actions," Anthony said ruthlessly.

"There's nothing wrong with Stacy," Laurie tried to reason with his brother. "She's just lonely."

Anthony sat forward and held up one hand impatiently. "Spare me the sad story, if you please. She could have many friends. Children her own age. All she would have to do is change her behavior. But I do not wish to discuss it any further. Miss Eustacia Prescott is no longer welcome here."

He stood up and walked slowly around his desk, keeping his eyes down, so that he missed the look of defiance that Laurie gave him. How dare Anthony dismiss Stacy as if she didn't matter! Laurie kept silent but vowed loyalty to her forever.

Anthony reached his brother's side and put his arm around Laurie's shoulders with an easy friendliness, as if the earlier scene were forgotten. "Now that that is settled, you must tidy up. Mrs. Chetwin and Blanche have come for tea."

Laurie strove to copy his tone, for open defiance of Anthony would never accomplish anything. "I was thinking, Anthony," he said slowly. "I thought perhaps you might like me to take Mrs. Chetwin out to the gardens for a while."

"Whatever for?" Anthony asked, stopping and staring at his brother in real puzzlement.

Laurie smiled. "Oh, come now, Anthony, you needn't pretend with me. I know you must like to see Blanche alone sometimes."

A cold remoteness settled on Anthony's face in place of his former friendliness. "Blanche and I do not have that type of relationship," he said icily.

"Surely you must feel some attraction to her, since you intend to marry her," Laurie said incredulously.

Anthony was furious, but Laurie was too concerned to notice the warning signs.

"I do not need to hold a woman in my arms to know if she will make a suitable wife," Anthony retorted. "I have great respect for Blanche. She comes from good stock, is quite sensible, and is reasonably attractive."

"My God! You sound as if she were a brood mare for your stables!"

"And why shouldn't I choose a wife on those qualifications?" Anthony fumed. "I have had great success breeding horses. I trust I shall be equally successful with a family."

"But why not look for someone you can love?" Laurie pleaded.

"Love?" Anthony scoffed. "I saw one so-called love match, and it was enough for me, thank you. I don't think that either Father or Mother was very happy."

"Yes, but perhaps they weren't willing to adapt to one another," Laurie argued. "Or they weren't really suitable."

"That is precisely my point. Their 'love' blinded them to all that," Anthony said with awful finality. He pulled the door open. "I shall expect you in the drawing room soon." He closed the door after him with quiet restraint.

The quality that Blanche Chetwin admired most in others was decisiveness, and she had worked hard to achieve it in herself. She had spent several frustrated years as a child, impatient with her parents' inability to make even the smallest decisions. Finally, in desperation, she took over the running of the household. No one was even slightly upset by her actions. Her parents and her older brother were all delighted to be able to go their own ways and leave things in Blanche's capable hands.

When the time came for Blanche to choose a husband, she slowly and carefully scrutinized each suitor. She was looking not for someone who would allow her to make all the decisions but for someone as decisive as herself. She would run the household, while her husband would run the estate. It would be a highly efficient arrangement.

As soon as she met Lord Anthony Kendall, Blanche knew that he was what she had been waiting for. He did not waste time writing sonnets to her lovely brown eyes, or her thick brown hair, but admired her ability not to have taken a chill after they were caught in an unexpected downpour.

When Lord Kendall proposed, there was no mention of love, which Blanche would have scoffed at, but rather of the merger of two competent individuals into a totally efficient organization. It was all she had ever dreamed of.

"I thought we would have a large ball at the end

of the season and announce our engagement," Blanche said. They were having tea in the drawing room of Anthony's home. The cool formality of the furnishings was a perfect setting for Blanche.

"If that's what you would like," Anthony said, nodding in agreement. "But I don't really see a reason to wait."

Blanche, however, always thought everything through and had a reason for all that she did. "With all of the announcements at the end of a season, ours would be lost in the *Gazette*. It will be much better to tell everyone ourselves," she decreed.

Anthony shrugged, while Mrs. Chetwin nodded. "A ball would be nice," she said timidly.

Blanche's smile rewarded her mother for expressing an opinion, however hesitantly it was offered. Then she picked up a sheaf of papers that was lying in front of her.

"I've made up a guest list for your alfresco party and have decided on a menu." She went on to mention small details about the party they were giving in a few weeks, but Anthony was not listening. He was thinking about the things that Laurie had said a short while ago. Looking back, they were rather amusing.

Blanche was an attractive woman, tall and with an impressive figure. She was always dressed neatly, and her hair was perfectly arranged. No strand ever dared slip out of place. One thing she was not was a simpering little miss. The thought of taking her out to the garden to steal kisses was preposterous, although Anthony had no doubt that she would perform her wifely duties adequately, which was precisely as he wanted things. He was not looking for some cloying emotion that blinded people to their real suitability. Long ago he had realized that people who were ruled by their feelings were always hurt, for those emotions gave others too much power over them. He had vowed never to fall into that trap. The only person he truly cared about was Laurie, and even with him Anthony was careful not to let his feelings get in the way of his good sense.

As he thought back to their earlier discussion he noticed a sudden stillness in the room, warning him that something was wrong. He looked up quickly. Blanche was staring at him sternly.

"I do wish you would be kind enough to listen to me when I speak," she said forbiddingly. "I have gone to a great deal of trouble preparing for this party."

Anthony flushed slightly and bowed. "Do forgive me. I'm afraid that my mind wandered for a moment. I'm quite sure that all your plans are perfect in every way," he added, not so much mollifying her as stating the truth. That was why he was marrying her, because she knew exactly what to do and fit in so well with his household.

"Do you expect that your grandmother will attend?" Blanche asked, only partially forgiving.

"I doubt it," Anthony replied, shaking his head. "Since grandfather died she rarely goes into society."

Blanche had been about to pick up her cup of tea but drew back in surprise. "But she will attend our wedding, won't she?"

Anthony shifted uncomfortably. "I'm not sure." He hesitated, because that wasn't strictly true. He and his grandmother did not get along well, and he did not know if she would even acknowledge the invitation. "She doesn't go out much, you see," he said lamely.

Blanche was prepared to be quite affronted. "It will seem very odd if she doesn't attend the wedding of her eldest grandson," she pointed out. "It will look as if she doesn't approve of your choice."

"Oh, no," Mrs. Chetwin said quietly. "Maybe she just wouldn't know what to wear." She could think of many reasons for missing even an important occasion.

"Maybe, if I went to talk to her . . ." Blanche suggested thoughtfully.

"Oh, no," Anthony hurried to kill that idea. Blanche and his grandmother would not get along, and the old lady was bound to say something that would cause him problems.

Before Blanche could question him further, Laurie came in. Anthony could not remember ever being so glad to see him. "Laurie!" he cried enthusiastically. "Come join us." He moved over on the sofa to give his brother room.

"How nice to see you, Lawrence," Blanche said condescendingly. She poured him a cup of tea and let her mother carry it over to him. "I do hope you are well."

Blanche's lady-of-the-manor attitude made him feel like a guest in his own house, and he nodded sullenly at her. She pretended not to notice and turned back to Anthony.

"I do so admire how you have raised Lawrence," she said to Anthony as Laurie bristled with irritation. "I only wish Jeremy had his sense of responsibility."

"I'm sure that Jeremy will be fine," Anthony tried to reassure her. "He is twenty-five now and cannot expect you to help him run the estate forever."

"I know." Blanche shook her head sadly. "But I cannot help but fear that I have forgotten to teach him something, and that he won't know what to do after we're married."

Laurie grimaced in silence. He'd be willing to wager that Jeremy was planning to throw a huge party to celebrate being rid of his sister. Rather than listen to such fustian, Laurie turned in his place and stared out the window at the orchard.

He watched idly as the wind blew the branches of the trees, paying no attention to Anthony or his guests. A flash of white between the trees caught his eye, and soon Stacy came into view, running toward the house.

Thinking that her timing couldn't be worse, Laurie glanced over at his brother. He was still listening to Blanche and had not noticed Stacy. Laurie stood up slowly, hoping that he could ease his way over to the door before anyone would notice.

"More tea already?" Blanche asked him, assuming that he was coming over to get his cup refilled.

"Uh, no, thank you," Laurie mumbled, glancing at his still full cup. "I've had all I want." He looked around him nervously. "I was just going out to get some air."

"Nonsense," Anthony scolded. "You've hardly visited with our guests. Now, sit down, have some sandwiches, and relax." Mrs. Chetwin passed him a plate of watercress sandwiches as he sat down dejectedly.

As Anthony and Blanche resumed their conversation, Laurie glanced furtively out the window. Stacy was getting closer. He crammed the sandwiches into his mouth and washed them down with his tea. He was about to try to sneak out again, when Mrs. Chetwin noticed his empty plate.

"My, it's good to see a young man enjoy his food so," she said, smiling at him. To Laurie's horror she passed him another plate of sandwiches. He opened his mouth to refuse, but Anthony was glaring at him, so he took them with a weak smile.

Afraid now to check on Stacy's progress, Laurie fatalistically ate the sandwiches, expecting her to burst into the room at any moment. When she still hadn't appeared by his last bite, he decided to make one last effort to leave.

Keeping his eyes on Anthony, who seemed quite engrossed with Blanche, Laurie put his cup on the table and stood up. As he rose to his feet his leg hit the cup, which was balanced on the edge, and knocked it to the floor. It shattered, spilling the remains of his tea onto the rug.

"Oh, I'm sorry," Laurie cried, staring down at the mess.

Anthony looked annoyed. "Don't just stare at it. Ring for someone to clean it up."

Laurie looked blankly at his brother for a moment, until the realization set in. This was his chance. "No, I won't ring," he cried. "I'll get someone." He turned and fled out the door to the terrace as if it were the natural place to find a maid.

Hurrying across the lawn, Laurie met Stacy in the courtyard, where they were out of sight of the drawing room. He was appalled by her appearance. Her face was pale, while her eyes were red and swollen, as if she had been crying. Her whole body was trembling, and she was out of breath from running.

"Oh, Laurie, I must talk to you," she cried, rushing toward him. She threw herself into his arms and sobbed, while he looked nervously around, expecting Anthony to pop out of the bushes at any moment.

"Let's go where we won't be disturbed," he suggested, leading her away from the house. He protectively kept his arm around her as he watched for his brother.

They went past the barn and into an old carriage house. It was dark and quiet inside. He led her over to a dusty trunk that lay near a wall, and they sat down. The only light filtered across the room from the door and didn't quite reach them, so Laurie could not see her face clearly. He thought that she had stopped crying.

"Now, tell me what's wrong," he said gently, taking hold of her hand.

In a low voice Stacy told him about Mr. Barlowe's visit and her surprise at seeing Mr. Palmer. Her voice broke slightly as she recounted everyone's pleasure at the brooch he had given her.

Laurie frowned in the pale light as he noticed the expensive brooch pinned to her dress. There was something almost obscene about its rich elegance compared to the childish dress on which it rested. As he heard her story a wave of horror washed over him. He could not bear to think of her in such a situation.

"He's a horrible old man," she cried, "but they are going to make me marry him. There's nothing I can do about it." She covered her face with her hands and wept.

Laurie awkwardly put his arms around her. In his growing awareness of her as a young woman, he was no longer at ease with her. His hands timidly patted her back, trying to ease the terrible sobs that shook her body. Slowly she seemed to be getting herself under control again.

"Does Tessie know how you feel?" he asked, once she could speak.

Stacy stayed comfortably within his arms, her head resting against his chest. "You know what she's like," she sighed. "She would never stand up to Mr. Barlowe for me."

Laurie nodded, only half-listening. He had never before held a girl in his arms and was finding it a delightful experience. Added to this warm feeling was the knowledge that she had come to him. She was a woman now and had come to him, as a man, for help. She was depending on him. His arms tightened possessively as the answer came to him.

"I suspect Tessie is right, that Mr. Barlowe can force you into marriage. The good part, though, is that once you are married, he has no more control over you."

Stacy shrugged in confusion, not seeing how that would help her.

"There's only one way out," Laurie went on. "We must elope!"

Stacy pulled away from him abruptly, looking up at him as if he had lost his mind. "Elope?" she squeaked in astonishment. "We couldn't do that!"

Laurie was hurt by her immediate refusal. "Why not?" he pouted. "Would you rather marry your fat Mr. Palmer? That seems to be the choice you have. Me or him."

Stacy stared at him uneasily. "It seems like such an important decision," she said hesitantly. "I don't feel prepared to marry anyone."

Laurie took both her hands in his and held them tightly. "But you must, don't you see? Mr. Barlowe can force you to marry Mr. Palmer, but if you marry me, you'll be safe from him."

Stacy still said nothing, so Laurie went on. "It's the only way I can help you," he said quietly. "And as far as I can see, it's the only way you can escape from Mr. Barlowe."

"I just don't know," Stacy said, a frantic note in her voice. "But I do know that Anthony would never approve."

"Anthony!" Laurie cried, jumping to his feet. "I don't need Anthony's permission to do anything! I am not a child!" Wasn't this the very thing he had just been telling his brother, and wasn't this the very way to prove it?

He turned back to Stacy, determined to win her agreement. "I love you, Stacy," he said quietly, bending to pick up her hand. He kept his eyes on it rather than her face, his voice betraying his nervousness. "I may not have all the fancy words of older men, but I really do care about you and want you to be happy."

Stacy found herself unable to speak, she was so moved by his words. She finally had someone who really cared about her, someone she could belong to.

Stacy threw her arms around his neck and hugged him close. Tears streamed down her cheeks. "I love you too, Laurie," she whispered brokenly. "I would be very happy to marry you."

CHAPTER THREE

It began to rain soon after the old carriage left the Kendall estate and headed north. It was not a hard, driving rain that would slow traveling, but it was enough to make the occupants of the carriage uncomfortable.

Water ran freely down the inside walls of the coach, for the roof leaked. The leather flaps that covered the windows managed to keep out the rain, but they also kept out the fresh air. The carriage had smelled musty when they left, but with the added flavor of the dampness, the odor was indescribable.

As if all that weren't enough, the coach was badly sprung and bounced from one rut in the road to another with bone-jarring accuracy. Stacy clung helplessly to a handle on the side.

"Are you sure that we should be doing this?" she asked Laurie through the darkness.

"Of course I am," he said, but his voice sounded less confident than it had that afternoon. Stacy felt him move over to her side of the carriage, and a moment later he took her hand.

Maybe she had been too hasty, Stacy thought. It was true that at dinner that night everyone acted as if she and Mr. Palmer were betrothed, but maybe that was because she had not been firm enough. Perhaps she should have tried to explain to Mr. Barlowe just how she felt.

The carriage went over another rough patch of bumps, and Stacy pulled back a flap to look out the window. Were they still on a road? She could see nothing but vague shapes, and aside from the noise of the carriage she heard only the sound of rain falling on the leaves. She let the flap fall back into place.

"I hope Anthony doesn't find us," Laurie said gloomily. At the mention of his brother's name he dropped Stacy's hand guiltily. "I don't see how he could, though," he laughed, trying to sound confident.

"Did you leave him a note?" Stacy asked.

Laurie shifted uncomfortably on the seat. "I didn't

want him to worry," he said defensively. "And he would if he didn't know where I was."

Stacy smiled at his defiant tone. "I left one too," she told him. "But it wasn't because I didn't want anyone to worry. I did it because I was furious at all of them. I said it was terrible that I should prefer to trust my future to a neighbor than to those people who are supposed to be concerned with my well-being and happiness."

"Oh, Lord," Laurie moaned. "Why did you have to tell them all that? Couldn't you have just said that you were going to spend a few days with a friend? Now they'll be after us for sure."

Stacy leaned back, closing her eyes and wondering if Laurie was regretting his offer. She did not point out to him that she had no other friends than him, for she did not want to remind him of her dependency. If he no longer cared what happened to her, she did not want to hold him with pity or guilt.

Laurie sneezed suddenly, and Stacy turned toward the sound, overcome with shame. How selfish she was, sitting here, wallowing in self-pity while Laurie was doing his best to help her. Dear, sweet Laurie. Deliberately, she reached along the seat until she found his hand. She took hold of it and squeezed it tightly.

"If Anthony does find us, you don't have to worry. I shan't allow him to yell at you," she assured him.

They rode in silence for almost an hour, enduring

the jolting and bouncing of the carriage, until Laurie could bear it no longer. Leaning out of the window, he called to the coachman to stop at the next inn.

"I hope there's nothing wrong with it," Laurie worried. "But all this bouncing doesn't seem right." He sat for a moment in silence. "It wouldn't have been right to take Anthony's good carriage," he tried to convince Stacy. "And I thought this one was in good repair."

"Don't worry about it," Stacy said. "It's not your fault."

"But what if it really delays us?" he pointed out. "What if Anthony catches up with us because of this?"

Stacy shrugged, refusing to become upset about it. "It just can't be helped."

Laurie was not satisfied with such logic, especially once they pulled into an innyard and discovered that one of their wheels was badly cracked.

"Yer lucky it didna come off when ya wuz goin' fast," an old stablehand said, shaking his head in wonder.

"How long will it take to be fixed?" Laurie asked anxiously.

The old man rubbed his fingers through his gray beard thoughtfully. "Oh, a day er so," he guessed. "Don't rightly know."

"A day!" Laurie cried. This was terrible! "Isn't there any way it could be done faster?" he pleaded.

"Not unless we wuz ta use a wheel off one of t'other carriages," he said, eyeing Laurie's expensive clothing with speculation.

"May we look?" Laurie asked eagerly.

"It'll cost ya more," the man warned.

Laurie scoffed at the expense. The possibility of avoiding Anthony's wrath boosted his self-confidence and gave him the authority he needed to take control of the situation. He escorted Stacy into the inn and ordered a late dinner for her.

"Don't worry about anything," he said with assurance. "Once the wheel is fixed we'll make up all the time we've lost. No one will catch up with us." He hurried back outside as a maid came to take care of Stacy.

She was shown into a small parlor in the back of the inn. It was a pleasant room, with clean curtains on the windows and a comfortable chair pulled up close to the fireplace, where a small fire burned. It provided just enough warmth to take the dampness out of the air.

Although she was exhausted, Stacy was too nervous to sit down and restlessly paced the room until a maid brought in her dinner. The girl put the tray on a small table in the corner, uncovering dishes of steaming pigeon pie, thick slices of ham, and freshly made bread.

Stacy smiled at the girl and reluctantly sat at the table, forcing herself to eat. She ought to be hungry, for she had eaten little dinner. Mr. Palmer's smiling face had ruined her appetite. But she could not really enjoy the food. She played with it for a while, eating about half of it, then finally sent the maid away with the rest.

She paced the room restlessly, wondering how long it would be before the wheel was repaired. It seemed she had waited for hours already, but in her restless state she was no judge of time.

Whenever she heard footsteps in the hall she would turn, expecting Laurie to come bursting through the door, but each time the steps trailed off somewhere else until she was totally exhausted and drained of feeling.

Finally, too tired to fight, she sank into the chair by the fireplace, putting her feet up on a small stool and leaning back, her eyes closed. She was blissfully peaceful, and drifted off to sleep.

She dreamed that she was in a garden, hiding from Mr. Palmer. She could see him searching for her, but she was afraid to run. Finally, she saw Laurie far away from her and tried to hurry toward him, but the brooch on her dress weighed her down, and she went more and more slowly. Mr. Palmer was getting closer, and she called out to Laurie for help, but he wasn't there anymore. Anthony was in his place and was laughing at her.

Stacy's eyes flew open, and she sighed in relief. It had only been a dream. Yet even as she realized that, she heard someone at the door. *Thank God*, she thought, jumping up. Laurie was finished at last. They could go.

The door flew open. It was not Laurie, it was Anthony, and he looked as if he'd like to kill her.

"Oh, hello," she said weakly, stepping backward until she was up against a chair.

Anthony said nothing, but stepped into the room, closing the door behind him. His eyes were filled with hatred as he moved closer to her.

Stacy clutched her hands together and tried to keep from shaking. She was terrified but would not let him see it.

"What the hell do you think you are doing?" he asked her menacingly.

She fleetingly thought of pretending to misunderstand him, but she decided that her safest course lay in silence. She looked up at him, hoping he wouldn't hit her.

"What was the purpose of this little stunt? To show me that you have more power over Laurie than I do?"

Stacy shook her head wordlessly, her eyes never leaving his face.

"Well, I can assure you that your little game has failed." His eyes were icy as he looked around the room. "Get your things together. I'm taking you home."

"Where's Laurie?" Stacy asked timidly, her hands clutched tightly together.

"Laurie will stay here to have the coach properly repaired and will return with it tomorrow," he said impatiently. He strode over to where her things lay on a chair and fairly threw them at her.

"May I see him?" Stacy asked. Her reticule slipped to the floor as she fumbled with her cloak.

"No, you may not," Anthony shouted at her. He impatiently picked up the small purse and thrust it into her hands. "From this moment on, you may not see him again." Stacy stared at him in disbelief as he spoke in commanding, measured tones. "You have done your best to undermine my authority over him and to ruin his life. I have forbidden him ever to talk to you or see you."

Stacy became as pale as a ghost. "But you can't do that!" she cried. A life without Laurie! It was unimaginable! Her eyes filled with tears, and she shivered at the thought. She would have no one if she lost Laurie. "Please don't do this to me," she pleaded. She put her hand on his arm and looked up at him, her eyes blinking rapidly to free them of tears.

She thought for a moment that his eyes softened at her distress, but it must have been the tears blurring her vision, for suddenly he was shrugging off her hand.

"My mind is made up," he said harshly.

"I'll do whatever you say." She humbled herself

completely. "I won't go anywhere with him, but please let me talk to him sometimes."

He refused even to look at her, but stared straight ahead. "Do you have all your things?" he asked coldly. Without waiting for an answer he walked quickly to the door.

As they passed through the inn Stacy looked around, hoping to catch a glimpse of Laurie, but he was nowhere in sight.

"He is quite safe, I assure you," Anthony said, noticing her furtive glances. "The object of this trip was to save him from you, not to do him further harm."

Stacy blushed a deep red and followed his angry figure out into the yard. He called for his coach in a loud voice, and the stablehands rushed to do his bidding while she stood in miserable silence at his side.

The rain continued to fall, but either Anthony was unaware of it, or no drops dared touch him. Stacy was not so fortunate. In a matter of minutes her hair was plastered to her face, and the bottom of her skirt was splashed with mud. She knew that she looked as wretched as she felt, and she only wished that she had the courage to throw herself beneath the wheels of one of the carriages entering the innyard.

Anthony's carriage pulled up before them, splattering Stacy's feet. A coachman raced over to open the door. Stacy had put one foot on the step, and felt

Anthony take her elbow to help her up, when another carriage stopped close to them.

"Eustacia!" they heard someone call. Both she and Anthony turned toward the sound. Mr. Barlowe was hurrying across the innyard toward them, with Tessie following close behind him.

Seeing the concern in Tessie's face, Stacy forgot her earlier anger at the governess, remembering instead all the years of affection that Tessie had given her. After Mr. Barlowe's manipulations and Anthony's threats, Tessie seemed like a haven of safety and sanity. Tessie would surely stand by her once she really understood how Stacy felt about being forced into marriage.

Stacy ran the few steps to meet her and threw herself into Tessie's arms. Choking back the tears that threatened to overcome her, she pleaded with the governess to help her fight Mr. Barlowe.

"Please say you'll help me, Tessie," Stacy begged. "I can't fight him by myself." The tears began to roll down her cheeks, and Stacy sobbed uncontrollably.

Tessie's arms tightened around her charge as she tried to soothe Stacy. "It's all right now," Tessie said quietly. "We're here now."

Her words barely made sense to Stacy, though. "I didn't know what to do," she continued to sob. "I was so frightened."

Tessie just held her tighter and looked across at Mr. Barlowe. Stacy's words had not been very clear, but to Tessie and the lawyer there was only one way to interpret them.

Mr. Barlowe looked about him in distaste, then back at Anthony, as if he were included in the disgusting surroundings. "I find this all quite abhorrent, Lord Kendall," he said in his best professional voice.

"I would prefer to conduct this discussion elsewhere," Anthony said impatiently. "And at a more reasonable hour. I do not know about the rest of you, but I would much prefer to be in my bed right now."

At the mention of his bed, Tessie shrieked in outrage and pushed Stacy protectively behind her. Mr. Barlowe took a step forward. "We are not leaving here until this matter is settled," he insisted loudly.

Anthony was annoyed and did not bother to hide it. "What is there to settle?" he demanded. "I was just bringing the stupid child home."

Stacy did not like his description of her, and she glared at him over Tessie's shoulder.

"It's a little late to return her home now, isn't it, Lord Kendall?" the lawyer asked scathingly. "And I would hardly call a young lady of seventeen a child."

Anthony turned to stare at Stacy with a new horror in his eyes. "No, she can't be," he protested weakly. In a daze he left the lawyer's side and walked slowly over to her. He pulled her away from Tessie's grasp. His gaze traveled slowly down the length of

51

her body. "Are you that old?" he asked in a strangled voice.

Stacy nodded timidly, shrinking back from the look in his eyes. It was not violence in them that frightened her, but the total lack of any emotion. He appeared to have gone into shock.

Mr. Barlowe was unaware of Anthony's preoccupation, and his voice went on, gaining volume as he became more and more agitated. A crowd gathered around them.

"You carried this poor orphan child to this disreputable spot in the middle of the night, thinking she was alone in the world," the lawyer accused. "You ruined her reputation, yet have the effrontery to tell me that she is a stupid child and you are returning her home. Well, sir, she is not alone. Her own dear parents chose me to be her guardian, and I shall not abuse the sacred trust they put in me."

Stacy looked at the lawyer in complete bewilderment, wishing he would end his ravings so they could leave. She turned to Anthony, thinking he had not been at a loss for words earlier, in the parlor of the inn, but he was watching Mr. Barlowe in stunned silence.

The lawyer felt the sympathies of the crowd were with him and pulled himself up to his full height. "You have stripped this child of her good name," he cried, "and must replace it with your own. I insist that you marry her."

CHAPTER FOUR

"This is ridiculous," Stacy grumbled as she squirmed uneasily on the edge of her chair and looked across the cheerless parlor at Anthony. Sounds from the streets of London filtered into the room, but neither of them showed any interest. "I don't see why you didn't tell Mr. Barlowe the truth," Stacy continued.

Anthony was as ill at ease as she was, but pretended to study intently a figurine from the table next to him. He put it down with careful precision before he turned back to Stacy.

"And what would that have gained?" he asked her with exaggerated patience. "Would it have been better if he knew that it was Laurie who compromised you, not me?"

Stacy shrugged. "At least you would not have been involved."

Anthony snorted in disgust and rose to his feet. He never could be patient with her for long. "Barlowe was determined to get you married. Do you really think I would have stood by while he ordered Laurie to marry you?"

Anthony's voice rose as he became agitated. He turned, seeking release for his anger in movement, but immediately bumped into a footrest. He kicked it out of the way, but there just was no space for him to walk around. The room was too small and confining. He threw himself back into his chair.

"What could you have done to stop it?" Stacy asked curiously, ignoring his outburst.

"Just what I intend to do now," Anthony growled at her. "Find some other fool to marry you."

Stacy leaned forward. "How are you going to do that?"

"Barlowe wants you wed," he reminded Stacy. She nodded impatiently. "But I don't think it matters to him who the bridegroom is. As long as you are married within the next few months, you could wed whomever you want."

"But why then—?" Stacy began, only to have Anthony cut her off.

"Right now he thinks that you are my fiancée and, therefore, under my control."

Stacy looked militant suddenly, but he went on,

not noticing. "He has agreed that the whole episode at the inn should be kept secret, for your sake, and that you may be presented to society by my grandmother before we announce any engagement. During that presentation you must make sure that you meet another that you prefer, and I will graciously step aside. As long as you are married soon, he won't ever learn of Laurie's involvement."

"And what if I don't choose someone else?" Stacy asked.

A look of irritation crossed Anthony's face, but he made a visible effort to control it. "Surely you must see it's in your best interests," he pointed out reasonably. "Since you are being forced into marriage, wouldn't it be best to marry someone you like?"

Stacy nodded, conceding that point. "But why should your grandmother agree to this?" she asked, looking around the drab room. Its unwelcoming atmosphere was a sure sign to her that she would not be wanted there.

"She'll be happy to help," Anthony assured her. He rose to his feet and paced the room restlessly, taking great care to avoid the furniture. "Not that I am going to tell her everything. I'm just going to ask her to take you about and introduce you to some of her friends. Some of them must have eligible relatives."

Stacy pulled at a strand of hair that had slipped from its pins. "It seems so dishonest," she said in a worried tone. "I don't mind tricking Mr. Barlowe, but to lie to your grandmother . . ." She shook her head slowly. "I thought that gentlemen were supposed to be honorable and not lie and cheat."

Anthony was stunned that she should imply such a thing about him. "I am not doing anything wrong," he insisted. "As for not telling the whole truth, I think that the situation is desperate enough to justify it."

Stacy jumped to her feet, her eyes blazing with anger. "I see," she said, barely controlling the desire to shout. "Even dishonor is preferable to having me in your family."

"That's nonsense," he snapped. "In spite of Barlowe's dramatics, I don't consider myself bound to you in any way, because I never compromised you. I am already betrothed to a fine woman, and it is to her that I owe my respect and loyalty. I am quite honorable in my dealings with her, I assure you. I am part of this masquerade only to save my tenderhearted brother from the consequences of your foolishness. Once you are tied to some idiot, I shall be quite delighted to wipe my hands of you." His eyes flashed quickly over her. "Although I don't know how we'll find anybody else willing to marry you when you look like a quiz and yell like a fishwife."

Stacy's mouth opened and closed furiously in a futile attempt to strike back, but she was so angry that no sound came out. In wild frustration she looked about for something she could throw at him, but as she reached for a Sèvres vase on the table next to her, the door opened behind her.

Both Stacy and Anthony turned at the same time and saw a tiny old woman in the doorway. She was leaning heavily on a cane, frowning intently as her eyes flashed around the room. Before she could speak, Anthony rushed over to her side and bent down to kiss her wrinkled cheek.

"Grandma, you're looking wonderful," he enthused, putting his arm around her shoulder, while Stacy watched in disbelief. "Let me help you to a chair," he offered solicitously.

Lady Elinor Slipwood pushed him away rudely. "I'm not in the grave yet," she snapped at him, and made her way across the room with slow, painful steps.

Stacy looked on in agony. This was the woman that Anthony expected would introduce her into society?

Lady Elinor finally made it over to a chair and lowered herself into it, grimacing all the while. Once she was settled, she turned her penetrating gaze on Stacy for a long moment, then looked back at her grandson.

"Well, what do you want now? And who is that drab-looking chit sitting in my hallway?" she asked impatiently. He was still standing by the door, though his eyes had followed her across the room.

Stacy fully expected Anthony to make some feeble excuse for their presence and quickly leave, but he cleared his throat, squared his shoulders, and walked briskly over to the chair before his grandmother. "I'm here on an errand of mercy, Grandmother, to ask your help for this unfortunate girl." A dramatic wave of his hand indicated Stacy. "The young woman you spoke of is her maid who accompanied us down to town.

"Miss Prescott, or Stacy as she prefers, lives on the estate next to mine. The poor child was orphaned as an infant and has been living a wretched life until now." His voice was oozing sympathy and concern. "She needs a chance to see things, meet people, perhaps even make an eligible connection." He stopped speaking but continued to look at his grandmother, hopefully keeping that touch of sadness in his eyes.

"Oh, don't try to cut a wheedle with me, Anthony." His grandmother's cynicism broke his spell. "What are you hoping to gain from all this?"

Anthony jumped to his feet, looking hurt. Stacy quickly swallowed a laugh. "How can you ask such a thing?" he cried. "The only thing I want is to see this child happy and settled in a decent sort of life." He struck a pose so full of sincerity that Stacy began to laugh.

Lady Elinor turned and looked at her. Stacy tried to turn her laughter into a cough, but the old lady was not deceived.

"It seems that the object of your charity doesn't quite agree with you," she commented dryly. "It's a good thing you never took up the stage. Your performances tend to lack credibility." She gestured to the chair he had abandoned. "Now sit down and tell me why you are really here."

Anthony warred briefly within himself, but he gave in and sat down. "I already told you the truth," he insisted. Her eyebrows raised slightly, but she said nothing. "I was hoping that you would present her to society. Dress her, take her to a few parties, that sort of thing."

"Are you planning on marrying her?" his grandmother asked bluntly.

Anthony jumped to his feet. "Good God, no!" he cried in horror. "All I want to do is get the stupid chit out of my hair!"

Stacy could be silent no more. She flew to her feet. "Nobody asked you to interfere," she pointed out loudly. "I wouldn't be 'in your hair' if you'd just kept out of it."

"And give you free rein to ruin everybody's life, I suppose!" Anthony shouted back.

"You're just angry because you want to run everything," Stacy argued. "You can't bear it if someone makes a decision without asking for a share of your overpowering wisdom."

"I saw precious little sign of any intelligence in

your behavior over the past few days," Anthony countered.

A quiet cough from Lady Elinor reminded them of her presence. Anthony turned very red and tried to regain his former concerned appearance. Stacy walked over to the nearest chair and threw herself into it. She did not try to maintain any semblance of dignity or decorum but leaned back, folding her arms, and looked crossly at Anthony.

A new twinkle had appeared in Lady Elinor's eye as she turned to her grandson. "Your 'poor child' seems to be fighting your charitable concern. I think, perhaps, we would do better without you."

Anthony stared at his grandmother, her dismissal of him taking him by surprise. "Does this mean that you will do it?" he stammered.

"I shall consider it after I've talked with the young lady." Lady Elinor was reluctant to commit herself. "If I do," she warned, "I shall expect you to escort us when we require it."

"Of course, of course," Anthony agreed readily.

"And attend any little gatherings that I might give."

"Certainly." Anthony waved aside her stipulations. He got up and moved toward the door. "Just let me know when and where you want me. I'll be there, I promise." He opened the door and, after bowing quickly to the two ladies, left.

Lady Elinor stared for a moment at the closed

door. "Fool!" she muttered, then turned to Stacy. "I think what we both need is a cup of tea."

Before Stacy could move, the old lady was on her feet. She walked briskly across the room and rang for a footman. Once he had come and gone, she turned back to Stacy. "Now that should . . ." She stopped as she saw that Stacy was staring at the cane still leaning against her chair.

"Oh, that." She grinned sheepishly. "I only use that for Anthony's benefit. I was hoping it might discourage him from whatever plan he had in mind for me this time."

Stacy stood up nervously. "If you would rather I left . . ."

"Oh, sit down." Lady Elinor laughed as she moved back to her chair. "Ever since my husband died four years ago, things have become very dull around here. Edmund and I used to have such fun together, he was so wild and impetuous. He made life tremendously exciting. In fact, he was so different from Anthony's dullness that the two of them couldn't be together without arguing. He wanted Anthony to be happy and was convinced that he had to break out of that controlled shell of his to enjoy life." She shook her head sadly, as if to chase the memories away.

"You can see why I had never thought Anthony would come up with something fun." She leaned forward and whispered confidentially. "I was afraid that he was going to badger me about meeting that frozen stick of a fiancée of his. Have you met her?" she asked.

"No." Stacy shook her head uncertainly.

"Well, I have," the old lady snorted. "And no great pleasure it was, either. I have no desire to become friendly with her or her family. Can't see why Anthony does," she added.

"Maybe he loves her," Stacy offered timidly.

Lady Elinor made a rude sound as the footman returned with their tea, but she abandoned the subject and pushed a plate of cakes over to Stacy. After they each had a cup of tea, Lady Elinor leaned back in her chair.

"Now tell me the truth," she said eagerly. "I know that Anthony isn't doing this out of the goodness of his rocklike heart." She looked thoughtful suddenly. "If this town bronze isn't to be acquired for his sake, is he doing it for Laurie?"

"For Laurie?" Stacy choked on the cake she was eating.

Lady Elinor nodded. "Is he hoping for a match between the two of you?"

Stacy's consternation turned to laughter. "Oh, no," she shook her head, tears forming in the corners of her eyes. "That's the last thing he wants. That's the very reason he rushed me off to you." She stopped suddenly, clapping her hand over her mouth as she remembered that Anthony hadn't wanted his grandmother to know that part.

Lady Elinor smiled gleefully. "I knew there was something interesting here. So you and Laurie want to marry, but Anthony refused his permission?"

"We didn't actually ask his permission," Stacy admitted, shifting uncomfortably. "We just eloped." Before Lady Elinor could express any opinion, Stacy rushed to tell her the rest. "We hadn't gone very far before Anthony and my guardian caught up with us."

"And your guardian didn't insist on an immediate marriage?" the old lady marveled. "He must not be very responsible."

"Oh, he did insist, and I guess I am betrothed. At least Mr. Barlowe thinks that I am. But there was this slight mix-up . . ." Stacy faltered. "You see, they didn't arrive together, and by the time Mr. Barlowe got there . . . well, I was with Anthony, and Mr. Barlowe thought—"

A shout of laughter from Lady Elinor interrupted her. "So you and Anthony are engaged," she cried. "No wonder he was upset. You won't be the kind of wife he thought he wanted."

"But I don't want to be his wife," Stacy hurried to point out.

"I can understand that. No sensible woman would, but once we take him in hand, he'll be more tolerable, you'll see." Lady Elinor rubbed her hands together in delight as Stacy watched her with concern. "I'm so glad that Anthony had the good sense to bring you here."

Stacy leaned back in her chair and pushed her short curls off her forehead. She had never thought dancing could be so exhausting. She looked up as Lady Elinor came into the drawing room.

"Monsieur LeBeau says that you are doing very well," she said, noting Stacy's weariness with a smile. "Perhaps, though, these lessons are for nothing. If dancing makes you so tired, then we must avoid any occasions where you might be expected to dance."

Stacy sat up and wrinkled her nose at the older woman. "I fail to see how anything could be more tiring than Monsieur LeBeau's instruction. According to him, I do nothing right. My feet are good only for stomping through the fields, I have no sense of the music, and it is too much to expect of any man to have to partner me for more than a quarter of a waltz, for guiding me is as difficult as pushing a heavy farm wagon through the mud."

Lady Elinor laughed outright. "I hadn't realized how hopeless you are. Perhaps we must warn everyone who asks you to dance that it might be dangerous."

Stacy did not share her humor. "It's all very well to laugh," she pouted, "but no one will want to dance with me, and you will be disgraced."

The older woman stopped laughing and looked over at Stacy sympathetically. "You will not disgrace anyone," she assured her. "You are just tired from all the dress fittings and the dancing lessons. Once they are over and the young men are pestering you, things will not seem so bad."

Stacy looked over at her skeptically but said nothing, then leaned back and closed her eyes. Lady Elinor had been wonderful to her. She had wholeheartedly thrown herself into Stacy's introduction to society, ordering vast amounts of clothes, hiring a dancing master, and supervising the trimming of her rebellious hair. She patiently instructed her in the ways of society, acknowledging that Tessie had been fairly thorough there.

Lady Elinor seemed vastly pleased with the result of her labors, but Stacy was not too sure that she could measure up to her expectations. It might have been different if Stacy could have looked in the mirror and believed that the lovely reflection was herself, but deep inside she still felt like the same frightened girl who had run to Laurie for help. She was so afraid that she would let Lady Elinor down and that that lady would want nothing more to do with her.

"I think I have just the surprise to cheer you up," Lady Elinor said, watching Stacy closely.

Stacy opened her eyes and looked at her. She showed remarkably little curiosity.

"Why don't you go out into the garden?" Lady Elinor suggested.

Stacy stood up and walked across the room to the doors that opened into the small walled-in garden behind the house. She saw someone sitting on one of the benches, and, her curiosity overcoming her lethargy, she stepped outside.

The young man stood up, and Stacy could see him clearly.

"Laurie!" she cried happily, and sped along the path to his side. Impulsively she threw her arms around his neck and hugged him. "What are you doing here?"

Laurie seemed relieved at her greeting and took her hand as they sat down on the bench. "Oh, Stacy, I thought you'd be furious with me," he sighed. "After the way I let you down . . ." He shook his head.

"Oh, Laurie," she cried. "You never let me down. It wasn't your fault that Anthony caught us."

Laurie looked down at his hands. "I should have planned it better," he said remorsefully. "And then when I heard that your guardian was going to make you marry Anthony, I was just sick. I know how you hate him, and you were going to have to pay for my irresponsibility for the rest of your life!"

He sounded so dramatic that Stacy had to laugh. "Knowing how Anthony feels about me, you should have known that he would fight the idea," she said dryly.

"But how can he?" Laurie asked.

Stacy shrugged. "He says his commitment to Miss Chetwin comes before anything forced on him by Mr. Barlowe. So I'm here with your grandmother to find a husband."

"I will still marry you if you want," Laurie offered bravely. He looked at her, suddenly noticing her new appearance. "I say, you look different."

Stacy laughed at the stunned tone in his voice. "I am still me."

But Laurie was not convinced. "You look like you belong at parties and drinking tea, instead of out riding with me. I don't think you need me anymore."

"Oh, Laurie," Stacy sighed, putting her arm through his. "I'll always need you. You are my very special friend, and always will be."

"But you aren't going to marry me, are you?"

Stacy sighed and looked at him sadly. She did not want to hurt him, but she knew he deserved the truth. "No," she said quietly. "I think I knew when we were eloping that it was the wrong thing for both of us, but I was so frightened I couldn't see any other way out. I'm not so afraid now, just a little nervous about the future, and I realize that I care too much about you to let your happiness be sacrificed."

She could tell from his puzzled frown that he did not understand. "If you care about me, then why . . .?" He shook his head.

"If we really loved each other enough to marry,

why didn't we ever think of it before?" Stacy teased him. "Marriage shouldn't come from desperation."

"Yes, but if you ever need me again . . ." Laurie said slowly.

Stacy squeezed his arm. "I promise that you will be the first one I turn to."

He seemed to relax suddenly, and Stacy suspected that he was glad to be released from his promise, especially since he happily changed the subject. "I was so glad when Grandmother invited me here," he said. "I've never been in London for much time before."

"You mean Anthony doesn't know you are here?" Stacy asked. Now it was her turn to look worried.

"No, I guess not," he said, totally unconcerned. "Grandmother showed me a London guidebook that she found and said that I can go about by myself and see the sights."

"Until Anthony sends you home," Stacy pointed out.

"He won't do that." Laurie was confident. "Grandmother's more than his equal in any argument."

Stacy smiled weakly and hoped that he was right.

"I think it's very strange that I received no invitation to your grandmother's dinner party," Blanche complained as she climbed into Anthony's curricle. "I will, of course, accompany you, but not to have

68

been sent my own invitation was quite remiss of her. She is fortunate that I haven't taken offense."

"She's been very ill and can barely walk. She probably just wants a small family affair," Anthony said, hoping to persuade Blanche the dinner party was not worth attending.

"Then I really should have been included." Blanche carefully arranged her skirts as Anthony allowed his horses to move back into the street. "I shall soon be a part of your family, you know. Besides, this girl she is introducing to society is not part of your family."

"Oh, she's just a plain dab of girl who's not worth bothering about," Anthony said impatiently. "The only reason grandmother took pity on her was because she's a close family friend, and since we haven't announced our engagement . . ." Anthony's voice drifted off meaningfully as he maneuvered the carriage around two dogs fighting in the street. He knew that Blanche was not pleased, but luckily some acquaintances were approaching in their carriage, and she chose to greet them rather than continue their argument.

Anthony was not sorry to drop the subject of Stacy, but he was curious about how she and his grandmother were progressing. It was two weeks now since he had brought Stacy there, and he had heard nothing from them but an invitation to a dinner party in a few days.

Blanche continued to greet those in passing carriages, to the exclusion of any conversation with Anthony, until they were driving down Bond Street.

"I would like to stop at Hookham's, if it would not inconvenience you," she said with rigid courtesy. "I wanted to read Miss Burney's new book to see if Cecilia should read it once she has finished the set of chair covers for the dining room I want her to make."

Anthony pulled up close to the walkway, and his tiger jumped down and ran to the horses' heads. "You've taken quite an interest in Miss Frayne," he commented absently.

"Yes, I am considering her as a wife for Jeremy."

Anthony's eyebrows went up in surprise as he walked around to Blanche's side of the carriage. "Isn't that up to Jeremy and Miss Frayne?"

"Oh, you know Jeremy." Blanche shook her head in despair as he helped her down from the carriage. "He would never think of it on his own, and even if he did, he'd never be able to make a choice."

Anthony escorted Blanche into the lending library, where she quickly drifted away from him to a group of her friends. Not bothered in the least by this punishment, Anthony walked idly around the library in search of a quiet corner.

He found a deserted area, and began idly to scan the shelves for something of interest, when he heard a noise behind him. He turned and saw a young woman straining to reach a book above her head.

"Could I be of assistance?" he offered politely.

She turned to look at him, her blue eyes widening in surprise.

"I'm sorry if I startled you," he apologized. His eyes strayed from her white dress, trimmed with ribbons of the palest blue, to the soft little curls of reddish-brown that peeped from under her bonnet and fetchingly framed her face. He felt a surprising desire to touch the curls and see if they were as soft as they looked. He recalled himself with a start and looked back into her face, but her eyes were demurely downcast, and all he could see were glints of blue through the dark lashes.

"Was there a book that I could get for you?" he repeated.

"Oh, yes," she said softly, turning toward the books. She pointed out a large book just beyond her reach. "It's very good of you to help me," she said as he pulled the book from the shelf. She put her hands out to take the book, but he did not give it to her.

"It's covered with dust and much too heavy for you to carry," he said solicitously. "You'd get your lovely dress soiled." He began to walk toward the entrance of the library. She walked at his side, but much to his disappointment she kept her head down, and all he could see of her was the top of her bonnet.

He glanced down at the book he was carrying, and stopped suddenly.

"You are interested in the stars?" he asked in astonishment.

She looked up at him then, her eyes sparkling as if with some secret joke. "Oh, yes," she smiled. "I love trying to find the constellations from my window at night. And to think that all through history, people have been looking at the same stars." She smiled dreamily at him as her voice slowed. "It makes one feel like a part of the universe."

He frowned suddenly. There was something naggingly familiar about her, and he tried in vain to place her.

She realized that he was not listening to her, and she stopped speaking, turning away from him. There was a strained moment of silence. "I daresay it's all romantic nonsense on my part," she said in a brisk voice.

Anthony looked down at her bent head, frowning in concern that his inattention had hurt her feelings. "I am sorry if my attention wandered," he said slowly, "but I have the strangest feeling that we have met before. Although I cannot believe that I would forget someone so lovely, if we had."

"I suppose that we might have," she said shyly, looking up at him for a moment, her whole face alive with a dazzling smile that took his breath away.

Then suddenly the bonnet hid her radiance from him again.

They walked in silence, passing small groups of people, until they were near the front door. Anthony looked about him questioningly. "Are you here with someone?" he asked.

Before she could answer, a familiar voice was heard behind them. "Imagine you two meeting here," Lady Elinor cackled.

Anthony turned around slowly, his hands tightening around the book he was carrying, and saw his grandmother's smiling face before him. She was looking at the girl at his side.

"Did you find the book you wanted, Stacy?"

Anthony's eyes reluctantly followed his grandmother's. This lovely girl could not be that hateful termagant! She was smiling back at him with unholy glee in her eyes. Of course, it was she.

"Anthony was kind enough to help me with it," she said, smiling in all innocence.

Anthony sucked in his breath, trying to keep under control the growing rage he felt. How dare this hoyden make a fool of him! And how could he have thought she was attractive? She was just as outrageous as she had ever been. He stifled a desire to choke her or throw the book at her, and merely looked at them both coldly. His grandmother ignored it and gave him two more books.

"You might as well carry them all," she laughed, and started toward the door.

"Might I ask the purpose of this little joke?" Anthony whispered harshly to Stacy as they fell in step behind Lady Elinor.

Stacy looked up at him, her face reflecting her surprise. "There was no joke intended," she assured him. They passed through the door and out into the street. Their carriage was waiting a few steps down the street. "I was going to tell you who I was," Stacy continued, "but, though you looked like the Lord Anthony Kendall I know, you certainly did not act like him. I thought it might be your double, not you."

She smiled sweetly up at him as a footman helped Lady Elinor up into the carriage. "I know I musn't introduce myself to strange men, so I thought it best to wait until I found out just who you were." She climbed up and sat next to the old lady. Anthony continued to glare at them.

"Make sure you come for my dinner party," Lady Elinor reminded him. "And stop scowling so. You'll frighten the horses." She nodded to the coachmen, and they pulled away.

As he watched the carriage disappear among the traffic on the street Anthony heard footsteps behind him. "Was that your grandmother?" Blanche demanded. "Why didn't you tell me she was here? She will be offended that you didn't present me." Blanche squinted her eyes and peered in the direction the carriage had taken. "I thought you said she was ill and could barely walk."

"She seems to have made a remarkable recovery," Anthony said dryly as he turned away from the street.

CHAPTER FIVE

Stacy stood still while Mary put the final touches on her hairstyle. Since her hair had been cut short, and curled naturally, Stacy did not understand how Mary could spend more than an hour arranging it. When she was allowed to look in the mirror, though, Stacy was amazed at her appearance.

Her reddish-brown curls seemed to fall naturally into place around the tiny yellow rosebuds that Mary had secured there. While Stacy stared into the mirror, Mary helped her into her dress. It was a soft crepe, in the palest of yellows and trimmed with narrow satin ribbons in a darker shade. Mary took a small bunch of the yellow roses that were on the dressing table and pinned it to the waistband of the dress. A cascade of ribbons fell from the flowers and swayed gently as Stacy moved.

"Now this is 'ow I always thought ye should look," Mary said, stepping back from Stacy.

Stacy took no credit for her loveliness. "I never knew you had such talent, Mary," she marveled. She spun around in front of the mirror, watching the ribbons fly around after her. "I just hope that I can remember everything Tessie taught me."

"Ye'll do fine," Mary dismissed Stacy's fears, and opened the bedroom door for her. "One look at ye, and ye'll 'ave all sorts of fine gentlemen poundin' at the door."

Stacy shook her head with a smile and went out into the hall. Taking a deep breath she started down the stairs. She could hear voices in the drawing room, so some of the guests must have already arrived.

Not allowing herself to hesitate, she put on a bright smile and went into the drawing room. Laurie was the first person she saw, as he stood near the door.

"Laurie," she said, taking his arm. "You don't know how glad I am that you are here. I only hope that Anthony will let you stay. Have you seen him yet?"

She spun around as she heard a cough behind her. There was Anthony sitting next to Lady Elinor.

"Anthony thinks it is delightful," Lady Elinor told her. "But in any case, since he has always told me that I might invite Laurie whenever I choose, he can hardly object."

Anthony looked like he wanted to object very much, but the butler announced the arrival of some more of the guests, so he had to be content with a scowl. Stacy gave Laurie's arm a quick squeeze, then hurried over to Lady Elinor's side to meet her friends.

Dinner was a very small affair, as most of the guests were arriving afterward for a party. Besides Lady Elinor, Stacy, Anthony, and Laurie, there were two gentlemen: Sir Clifford Stockwell and Mr. Stephen Granger, and a friend of Lady Elinor's, Mrs. Sally Frayne, and her granddaughter.

Cecilia Frayne was a plain girl with soft brown hair and dark brown eyes. She seemed very timid but had a friendly smile, and Stacy was sure that she was going to like her.

The two gentlemen were more frightening. They were dressed so splendidly and seemed so sophisticated that Stacy did not think they could possibly want to meet her.

At the dinner table Stacy was seated between Mr. Granger and Anthony. Although she was glad to be near someone she knew, she thought Anthony would probably scold her or refuse to talk to her at all, but he was too well bred to display his feelings in public. He tried to be the perfect dinner partner.

"Are you enjoying London?" he asked her with cool courtesy once they were settled in their seats.

"I haven't seen much yet," Stacy pointed out. "So far, most of my outings have been to the dressmakers." She looked with interest at the platters of food that the footmen were carrying in.

"Yes, but how successful those outings have been!" Mr. Granger said. He was quite openly eavesdropping.

Stacy blushed and smiled at him uncertainly, not sure how to handle such compliments. "Thank you," she murmured.

"Oh, no," Mr. Granger argued. "Thank you, for giving us such beauty to gaze upon."

Anthony felt slightly nauseous, but Stacy just blushed a little more and looked down at her plate in confusion. A footman placed a serving of pheasant before her and covered it liberally with a dark wine sauce.

"I'm sure that Grandmother has planned some excursions for you," Anthony told Stacy rather sternly, annoyed that she had apparently fallen for Granger's flattery.

"Oh, but it won't be necessary for her to go to such trouble," Mr. Granger said smoothly. He waved aside a footman with a dish of parsleyed potatoes. "I would consider it an honor to take you wherever you would like to go. Perhaps we could go to Hampton Court one day soon."

"That would be wonderful." Stacy's face glowed with excitement.

"We could even get together a small group and stop for an alfresco luncheon at an inn," Mr. Granger went on to suggest.

Before Stacy could overwhelm him with her gratitude, Anthony broke in. "Miss Prescott is already committed to attend one alfresco party, so I doubt that she needs another one."

Stacy looked at Anthony in surprise. "I don't remember anything about an alfresco party," she said, trying to recall the plans Lady Elinor had spoken of. "Are you sure that it was approved by your grandmother?"

Anthony looked irritated. "I hardly think that she is likely to object to you attending a party at my home."

Stacy's eyes widened in surprise.

"Why, that sounds like a delightful idea," Mr. Granger enthused.

"Will you be there too?" Stacy asked excitedly.

Mr. Granger feigned shock. "Need you ask?" he cried. "For the rest of the season all you need do is look over your shoulder to see where I am."

Stacy blushed again in delightful confusion, while Anthony fiercely stabbed a piece of roast. What had possessed him to invite the chit in the first place? And now he was stuck with that fop Granger, too. Blanche would not be pleased.

Rather than watch Granger make a further fool of himself, Anthony turned to Mrs. Frayne, who was on his right. She, at least, knew how to conduct a proper dinner-table conversation.

Many more guests were arriving by the time the gentlemen returned to the drawing room; but Anthony was in no hurry to join the others and dawdled along the hallway, pretending to be interested in the portraits of his mother's ancestors that lined the walls.

He stopped in front of one sour-looking gentleman from the sixteenth century.

"I'll bet it was something he ate," someone said over Anthony's shoulder.

He turned around and saw Jeremy Chetwin gazing up at the portrait. Anthony looked back at it himself.

"Actually, it was because he married an actress, who ran through his fortune, then left him."

Jeremy shook his head. "Your family does seem to have trouble choosing wisely, doesn't it?"

Anthony looked at him in exasperation. "What are you doing here, Jeremy?" he asked.

Jeremy pretended to take offense at his question. He whipped a cream-colored card from his pocket. "Why, I was invited," he said haughtily. A sudden smile broke through. "I hear that these invitations were in great demand, though."

A look of annoyance crossed Anthony's face. How

was Blanche skipped but her brother invited? "I fail to see why—" he began.

Jeremy interrupted. "We unattached, handsome devils are in great demand, you know," he teased. Then, looking around him quickly, he leaned close to Anthony and spoke in a whisper. "Besides, I'm much nicer than Blanche is." He winked quickly as he straightened up.

Anthony had to laugh. Jeremy was impossible, never serious about anything. They went into the drawing room together.

Quite a number of people had arrived, and the room was fairly crowded. Directly across from the door, though, was a clear space, and everyone entering could see Stacy, Laurie, and Cecilia talking together.

"Who is the new beauty?" Jeremy whispered in awe.

Anthony tried to control his impatience. "She's a neighbor of mine. Grandmother is introducing her this season."

Jeremy turned to look at Anthony, disbelief clearly written on his face. "You live near her, and you're courting Blanche?" He shook his head. "Now I am certain that insanity runs in your family. Not that I'm complaining, mind you. I'd rather not compete with you."

"I thought you were interested in Miss Frayne," Anthony pointed out sternly.

"Come now," Jeremy laughed. "How can you even compare the two?"

Anthony looked across the room to where the girls were sitting. Stacy was talking quite animatedly, her face glowing. The sound of her laughter drifted over to them. He had to admit that she presented an attractive picture.

But Cecilia was attractive, too, although her beauty did not strike one at first glance. She had a pleasant personality and was easy to talk to.

"Cecilia has many fine qualities," Anthony said in her defense.

"But she has one major drawback," Jeremy pointed out. "Blanche is on her side." He straightened his cravat and pulled his coat to remove any wrinkles. "Now," he said, "are you going to introduce me to the vision, or must I introduce myself?"

Stacy was meeting so many people that she found it difficult to remember all their names. One particularly forbidding matron was bearing down on her, and Stacy tried frantically to remember who she was. Was she Lady Cresting or Mrs. White?

Just before the woman was close enough to speak, Stacy heard a quiet voice behind her. "She is Mrs. Sheridan, and that man in gray and green near Lady Elinor is her son Philip. Don't agree to anything she wants you to do."

Stacy glanced around her quickly and saw Cecilia

right behind her. The other girl winked and turned back to the conversation she was listening to, as Stacy greeted Mrs. Sheridan.

"It's so nice to meet you," the older woman said as she settled herself down next to Stacy. "My dear Philip was especially eager to get to know you better."

Stacy smiled at her uncertainly.

"He is hoping that he might have the honor of escorting you to Almacks one evening soon. With Lady Elinor, of course," she added.

"That would be up to Lady Elinor to decide," Stacy said slowly, amazed at the woman's boldness. "I don't even know if we are going to Almacks."

Mrs. Sheridan looked thoughtful. "Perhaps I could help you there. I'm sure that I could get you a voucher."

Stacy shook her head quickly. "You must talk to Lady Elinor about that."

Mrs. Sheridan patted Stacy's hand, and said with a smile, "You and Philip would make such a lovely couple." Looking up, she noticed Lady Elinor moving among the guests. "Perhaps I'll mention it to her now." She hurried across the room, leaving Stacy momentarily alone.

"She can be rather pushy," Cecilia said, taking the spot the other woman had just vacated. "As long as you don't come right out and agree with her, you're safe."

Stacy smiled at Cecilia in relief. "She thought Philip and I would make a lovely couple."

Cecilia nodded. "She thinks that about every new girl in town, before they get a chance to actually meet him."

Stacy looked at Philip Sheridan where he was standing across the room. He appeared to be ill at ease, but that was hardly a crime. "What's wrong with him?" she asked Cecilia.

"Besides the fact that he never bathes and has a hideous smell, there's only his habit of trying to grab at the nearest girl."

Stacy stared at her in disbelief. "He sounds charming," she said.

Cecilia nodded. "I was surprised to see him here, but your grandmother has been out of touch lately. He has some older brothers who are quite nice, but they're married now. She must have thought he'd be like they were."

Stacy looked across at him and shuddered. "Just keep away from him and you'll be fine," Cecilia advised. "If you do have to deal with him, mention his mother often. It keeps him respectable."

Stacy giggled at Cecilia's implication; then she suddenly looked up and saw Anthony and another young man approaching.

She glanced over at Cecilia, about to ask her if she knew the young man, and was startled to see Cecilia blushing.

"Miss Prescott," Anthony said in a voice of sorely tried patience. "May I present Mr. Jeremy Chetwin? He was quite anxious to meet you."

Stacy looked up to greet him, when to her amazement the young man fell to his knees before her. "I am your undying servant, Miss Prescott," he proclaimed loudly, reaching for her hand and smothering it with kisses. "Your slightest wish is my command."

Stacy's first reaction was to burst into laughter at the look on Anthony's face. He simply could not believe that a sensible young man might be attracted to her. Stacy hid her amusement as she turned back to Jeremy.

"I truly do appreciate your sentiment," she told him, retrieving her hand, "but I do wish you would get up. You seem to be attracting a great deal of attention."

"Because you wish it, I will," he sighed and rose to his feet.

"Miss Prescott," Mr. Granger broke in, "I must warn you that Chetwin here is a scamp and a rascal, and totally untrustworthy." He reached down and took Stacy's hand, pulling her to her feet. "I feel it's my duty to rescue you from such bad company."

From off in the corner a piano began to play, and Lady Elinor hurried over to them. "Mrs. Patton has agreed to play for you, if you would like to dance."

"A delightful idea," Mr. Granger agreed, tightening his hold on Stacy's hand. "May I claim the first dance?"

As couples moved across the room to the space cleared for dancing, Lady Elinor stayed at Anthony's side. "Stacy seems to be doing very well, doesn't she?" she noted proudly.

He ignored her question and looked at the clock on the mantel impatiently. "I think I'll be taking my leave," he said. "I promised Blanche I would meet her at the Applewhites' function."

Lady Elinor was not ready to excuse him yet. As he started to move away from her she put her hand on his arm, holding him back. "I've been meaning to talk to you about that fiancée of yours," she said.

Anthony turned back hopefully. "You mean, I may bring her for tea one afternoon?" he asked.

"Well, I'm not sure." Lady Elinor hesitated, her hands fluttering about. "I thought we could discuss what would be an appropriate time and occasion."

Anthony forgot his impatience to be off. "I'm not sure what her schedule is," he hesitated, "but . . ."

Lady Elinor looked faintly scolding. "I never meant we should discuss it now," she said. "I have guests." Her hand waved vaguely around the room to remind him. "I thought if you could just stay until some of them leave . . ." She looked up at him beseechingly.

Anthony sighed, well aware that she had him in a trap. "All right, I'll stay."

His grandmother reached up and patted his cheek gently. "That's a good boy," she said. "Now why don't you go over and dance with Stacy?" She smiled sweetly at him and moved back to her other guests.

"I wouldn't take Chetwin too seriously," Anthony warned as he and Stacy went to take their places in the set. "He makes a lot of fancy speeches but rarely remembers them the next day."

The fact that Jeremy was a Chetwin was enough to make Stacy steer clear of him, but there was also the fact that she was sure that Cecilia was fond of him, and he barely even spoke to her.

Stacy glanced over to where Cecilia was talking with Sir Clifford. She was listening to him, but her eyes kept straying toward Jeremy as he flirted with Mrs. Patton's daughter, Amy. Jeremy Chetwin might be amusing, but he was also very rude. None of that excused Anthony's interference, though.

"I find him quite charming, thank you," she told Anthony obstinately, "and see no reason to suspect he might not be sincere. However, I do believe that I am old enough to recognize wild flattery."

"Well, you did seem to be taken in by it," Anthony uncertainly tried to excuse himself.

"I can't see that that's any of your concern," she said coldly.

The music started, and Stacy was relieved when the steps of the dance took her away from Anthony. Being in London made no difference. He still was as odious as ever. She rewarded all the other men in the dance with a dazzling smile, but she performed her steps with Anthony woodenly, resolving to stay as far from him as possible in the future.

CHAPTER SIX

"Do you realize that my brother was invited and I wasn't?" Blanche cried. She was dressed for riding and slapping her riding crop against her leg in agitation. "All of London must know by now that I was not included."

Anthony glanced over at Mrs. Chetwin, who seemed absorbed in her needlework, then back at Blanche. "I doubt that many people noticed," he said, and saw her lips tighten in anger. "Besides, Grandmother is trying to marry Miss Prescott off, so naturally she would choose many eligible men to include."

"I hope she does not feel that my brother is available," Blanche said haughtily. "His interests lie in another direction."

Anthony shrugged weakly, remembering Jeremy's conversation from the night before. "Cecilia was there too," he added.

Blanche seemed relieved that her choice for Jeremy's wife had been present to protect him.

Anthony moved hesitantly toward the door. "Shall we take our ride now?" he suggested hopefully.

Blanche nodded condescendingly and led him out of the room. She maintained her silence as they mounted their horses and headed toward Hyde Park, followed at a respectable distance by her groom.

Although she did deign to speak to people they passed, she did not even look in Anthony's direction, and he was beginning to feel annoyed. His anger was not directed toward Blanche, however, but toward his grandmother and Stacy. Since he had become involved with those two, Blanche had had to put up with quite a number of inconveniences. She had every right to feel angry. As his fiancée she had the right to expect his company and should not have to share it with some troublesome chit.

"Grandmother mentioned inviting you to her home," Anthony told Blanche as they entered the park.

Blanche stopped her horse and turned to him, a look of excitement on her face. Quickly forgiving

Anthony for all his offenses, she begged him for details. "When is it to be?" she asked. "It wouldn't have to be anything elaborate. In fact, something small and intimate would be better." She stared off in the distance, imagining the moment of triumph when Lady Elinor actually accepted her as a part of her family.

The Dowager Duchess of Wiltshire passed by in her carriage, and Blanche nodded absently in her direction, too engrossed in Anthony's news to notice her.

"I'm not sure when she had in mind," Anthony said nervously. "We didn't have time to discuss it."

The cold look returned to Blanche's eyes. "I thought you said she mentioned it."

"Oh, she did," he assured her. "And she wanted to make plans once her guests left, but when they did, she was just too exhausted. I'll be seeing her soon, and I'll arrange it."

Blanche was only partially soothed by his words. Lady Elinor had been a leader of society when she was younger, and there were still a great many people that looked up to her. It was an honor to be one of her confidantes, for she was very selective about her friends. Blanche stifled a sigh of aggravation, forcing herself to be patient. She was certain that once Lady Elinor met her, she would be immediately admitted to that elite circle.

They rode in uneasy silence around the park.

Blanche managed to maintain an image of cordiality, although Anthony did not test it too far.

They had made a complete circle of the park, when Blanche stopped her horse. "There's Jeremy," she told Anthony, her voice betraying her bewilderment. "I wonder who is in the carriage he's stopped by." She strained her neck to get a better look, but was blocked not only by her brother but by several other gentlemen on horseback as well. She turned instead to Anthony. "Do you know who it is?"

Anthony cursed under his breath. "It looks like Miss Prescott," he said, trying to keep the despair from his voice.

Blanche looked interested. "Your neighbor friend?" she asked. "I should like to meet her." She moved her horse forward, not waiting for Anthony.

Anthony ignored the sinking feeling in the pit of his stomach and followed close behind her. As they drew near, some of the others moved aside, making room for them.

Stacy was sitting with Mr. Granger in his carriage, but she was laughing and talking with Jeremy and two other gentlemen who had pulled alongside them. She was wearing a soft green dress with little sleeves, and a white bonnet tied with green ribbons. Her eyes sparkled as she laughed, and it was quite clear that her audience, including Jeremy, was entranced.

Stacy was delighted to see Anthony approaching. She had not forgiven him for his pompous attitude the night before, and recognized her opportunity for revenge.

"Anthony!" she cried out happily as he drew close. She held out a hand in greeting, as if she were delighted to see him. He took it warily, conscious of Blanche nearby.

Blanche pulled her horse up next to Anthony's and took note, with extreme disfavor, of Stacy's hand in Anthony's. She looked far from friendly, but Stacy pretended not to notice as Anthony made the introductions.

"Miss Chetwin!" Stacy cried with pleasure. "Why you must be Jeremy's sister! How wonderful to meet you!"

Blanche's eyes narrowed. "Jeremy?" she questioned, her voice rough with scolding.

Stacy giggled with embarrassment and threw Jeremy a playful look. "I mean, Mr. Chetwin."

"Oh, no," Jeremy protested. "I thought you agreed we could be friends." He sent his sister a look of annoyance that only served to aggravate her further.

"No, your sister is right," Stacy said sadly. "It is different with Anthony because we've known each other so long."

"Anthony?" Blanche's voice became even colder.

"Is that forbidden too? Oh, how I wish you had been at the party last night to help me with all these details!" Stacy said innocently, secretly laughing at

Anthony's murderous look. "Tell me, do you think I could call him Anthony in private?" Stacy looked up at Blanche, her eyes open wide in innocent questioning.

"It is not up to me to instruct you, Miss Prescott," Blanche said curtly. Nodding to her brother, she moved her horse away. "Shall we be going?" she said over her shoulder to Anthony.

He said his good-byes politely, but quickly followed her.

"She is hardly a 'plain dab of a girl,'" Blanche quoted him as they rode from the park. Her back was ramrod straight, her eyes glued forward. It is doubtful she would have recognized the Prince had he passed by.

"She was," Anthony said, but with little conviction. No one would believe that that lovely girl was the hideous creature he had brought to London a few weeks ago.

"Jeremy was supposed to go over the accounts with me this morning, but she has lured my poor brother away from his responsibilities," Blanche accused.

Anthony felt compelled to defend Stacy. "It's hardly her fault if he pesters her."

Blanche turned her head slightly to send him a frigid glare. "Jeremy would not pester a girl. He is far too quiet for that sort of thing." Her head returned to its former position.

Anthony shook his head. This was one argument he was not going to win, so he diplomatically remained silent. Instead, he spent his time planning what he would say to his grandmother and the troublesome hoyden she was sheltering.

Laurie walked along Oxford Street, looking about him eagerly. Everything in the city interested him. It was all so new and exciting. He still could not believe his good fortune actually to be staying in London, trusted to roam about without supervision.

His first stop would be the British Museum in Montague House, but along the way there was much to be seen, and his progress was slowed as he took in all the activity around him.

Peddlers were calling out their wares as they walked up and down the streets. Everything from ballads to oysters were being hawked.

He stopped to buy an apple from one hawkster and watched a housewife bickering with a knife grinder over his fee. A rabbit seller came by, swinging a large stick to chase away the pack of dogs that trailed along behind him. Laurie laughed as time after time the dogs swerved easily out of reach of the stick and quickly closed in again, the smell of the meat attracting them.

A sudden shout behind him caused Laurie to jump aside. He moved just in time as a woman threw a bucket of swill into the street where he had been standing. She laughed coarsely at his narrow escape, but he just smiled good-naturedly at her and moved along.

Laurie turned off Oxford Street reluctantly. The narrower streets seemed much less exciting, but he was determined to stick to his agenda. He went down one short street, then turned onto another. It was deserted, and his footsteps rang out loudly.

A carriage, coming the same way he had, turned into the street and passed him by, stopping in front of a house a few doors ahead of him. A young girl alighted from it and unloaded several large packages, piling them on the ground. She glanced up at Laurie and smiled shyly, then reached into her reticule to pay the driver.

As Laurie watched she handed something to the driver; he looked at it, then jumped down, obviously threatening her.

"But I haven't any more change," Laurie heard her cry. "That was what we agreed on."

The man muttered something and began to throw her bundles back in the carriage. She grabbed hold of his arm, trying to stop him, but he roughly shook her off, causing her to stumble.

"Stop that!" Laurie cried indignantly as he rushed forward, ignoring the fact that the driver was much larger than he was. He put himself between the girl and the man. "Surely there's no reason for such rudeness."

The man stopped and glared suspiciously at Laurie, who was experiencing a peculiar feeling in his bones as he realized how much bigger the driver was. He tried to swallow his fear and glared back at the man.

"I think it would be best if you went on your way," Laurie said, hoping his quiver of fear was not noticed.

Much to his relief and astonishment, the man did just that. He muttered an apology to the girl and retrieved the rest of her packages from the coach. Then he mounted the box and drove away.

Laurie watched as the carriage turned the corner and disappeared, amazed at what he had accomplished. He suddenly remembered the girl and turned around.

She, too, had been watching the carriage drive away, but turned to smile up at Laurie. He suddenly felt ten feet tall.

"Are you all right?" he asked solicitously.

"Oh, yes," she nodded. "But I don't know how to begin to thank you." Her voice was soft and musical. "You were so brave when you stood up to that bully." She looked up at him, her eyes wide in appreciation.

"It was nothing," Laurie assured her humbly. She was wearing a worn brown pelisse with a hood that covered her hair, but as she spoke to him it slipped back and revealed masses of soft blond curls. Laurie could not take his eyes off them.

The girl smiled at him again and bent to pick up her packages. Her movement jolted Laurie back to reality. "Let me help you," he cried, and took them out of her hands and from the walkway.

Blushing prettily, the girl put her hands to her cheeks. "You are just too kind," she exclaimed.

"Just show me where to take them," he offered gallantly.

She led him up the steps of a dilapidated house nearby. Fumbling in her reticule for a key, she unlocked the door and held it open for him.

"Is that you, Althea?" a voice from deep in the house called.

Althea smiled at Laurie. "You can just put them down in there," she said, pointing out a small parlor. Then she hurried over to the stairway. "Thomas," she called up it, "we have a guest."

Laurie put the packages down in the parlor and looked around him. The room had seen better days. The velvet draperies were faded and worn. The material on the small sofa and chairs was threadbare in spots, and there were water stains on the walls. It did not seem like a proper setting for someone as lovely as Althea.

"You will stay and have some tea with us, won't you?" Althea asked him. Seeing his hesitation, she added, "My brother will want to thank you for your help and would be so sorry to have missed you."

She looked so appealing, her blue eyes begging him to stay, that Laurie had no choice. He sat down in one of the chairs nearby. "I suppose I can spare the time."

Althea's face lit up with a smile as she sat down near him. "I would hate for you to have to run off before we even met," she said shyly, hardly daring to look at him.

Before Laurie could answer, a large, burly man in his middle thirties came into the room. Althea jumped up at his approach and rushed over to his side, drawing him closer to Laurie. "This is my brother, Thomas Johnson," she said. "Thomas, this young gentleman saved me from terrible unpleasantness today."

Thomas turned to look at his sister, his face creased with concern. "You should not go out by yourself," he cried. "This town is not safe, you know that." He turned to Laurie and extended his hand. "But I am forgetting myself," he apologized. "I worry so about her when she goes out that it makes me forget my manners. Thank you for your help, Mr. . . . ." His voice trailed off as he realized that he didn't know his name.

"Lawrence Kendall," Laurie told him as he shook the man's hand. "And it was nothing, really. I was honored to be allowed to assist her." He looked over at Althea, who stood in the protection of her brother's arm. She smiled at him again.

A middle-aged lady dressed in black carried in the tea tray, and they all sat down. As Althea poured the cups of tea, Thomas turned to Laurie.

"Are you any relation to the Lord Kendall I've read about in the newspaper?" he asked.

Laurie looked surprised. "That would be my brother, but why was he . . . ?"

Thomas started to laugh. "Oh, it was just in the society columns," he said. "Althea and I like to read them. We may never meet anyone in them, but we enjoy the things they do."

Laurie nodded uncertainly. He couldn't imagine Anthony ever doing anything the newspaper would find interesting, even for its society column.

"Mr. Kendall," Althea said softly.

Laurie looked up to see her holding out his cup of tea. He blushed and took it with a smile. She smiled back shyly, then handed her brother his cup.

Thomas stirred his tea thoughtfully for a moment. "Lawrence," he said suddenly, "I'm going to take advantage of your kind nature, because I feel as if I know your brother and can trust you." He put his cup down and looked at Laurie seriously.

"Althea and I have just recently moved here, because I have business to conduct in the city. When I am away from home, I worry a great deal about her, especially if she has to go out for some reason."

He waved his hand in emphasis. "You saw for yourself what can happen. I would feel so much better about leaving her if I knew that you were close by, that you could take her about where she would want to go."

"Oh, no, Thomas," Althea protested quietly. "That would be asking too much of Mr. Kendall. He has been so kind already. You cannot expect him to give up his time any further."

"But I would consider it a pleasure," Laurie told them quickly. "I can understand your concern. In fact, if I didn't offer my protection, I should worry also."

Thomas looked relieved. "We are truly in your debt," he said gratefully.

Laurie found it embarrassing to be thanked for something that would be a dream come true for him. He finished his tea quickly and stood up. "When would you like me to call for you again?" he asked Althea. "Tomorrow?"

"Oh, no," she shook her head. "I couldn't take up so much of your time. Perhaps on Thursday?" she suggested tentatively.

"That would be fine." Laurie bowed to her and her brother, hiding his disappointment that he would have to wait three days to see her again. Amid repeated cries of gratitude, Laurie made his exit. He continued on his way to the museum, but he feared he would find it quite flat now.

* * *

"What do you mean she isn't back from her drive yet?" Anthony raged at his grandmother. "I cannot wait about here all day for her. There is a new mare at Tattersall's that I want to see, and I have an appointment at Manton's later this afternoon. I had expected you to have more control over her than this."

"Don't be such a nodcock, Anthony," Lady Elinor said with total unconcern. She was picking out stitches in a tapestry she was making, and not affording him much of her attention. "She has only been gone for a short while, and I trust Mr. Granger to return her within a proper length of time."

Anthony threw himself into a chair across from her and glared at her. He moodily watched his grandmother for a few minutes. "How are you feeling today?" he asked her innocently.

"Just fine," she said, smiling at him briefly before returning to her work.

"Good," he said, leaning forward slightly. "Then we can discuss your invitation to Blanche."

Lady Elinor leaned back in her chair suddenly, resting her head against the back of the chair and closing her eyes. "When I said I felt fine," she told him, "I meant fine, considering how tired I am from the party last night." She opened one eye a small slit, but he was watching her suspiciously, so she quickly closed it. "I'm sure this discussion could wait until I'm stronger."

"This is all an act, and we both know it," Anthony scolded. "Aren't you a little old to play such games?"

Lady Elinor sat up again, looking slightly put out that her ruse had not worked but still in good spirits. "I only do it because I can't really believe that you mean to marry that girl." She shook her head at the thought.

"You have this blind prejudice against Blanche, but you've never even met her," he said. "Why not invite her for tea? You'd see she's very nice."

His grandmother snorted her disbelief. "I did meet her once, last year, and was not too impressed with her."

Anthony looked surprised. "Well, give her another chance," he suggested hopefully.

Lady Elinor put down her needlework. "You cannot really mean to marry her," she repeated. "Surely you aren't in love with her."

"Of course not," Anthony scoffed.

"Then why rush into marriage? It's hard enough to live with someone even if you love them, but impossible if you don't."

"Is that the advice you gave my mother before she married?" he asked scathingly. He rose to his feet and walked over to the window, blindly staring out at the small garden behind the house. "You must have had her convinced that she'd live happily ever after, since she was marrying for love." He could not keep the bitterness from his voice.

"Actually, I was against the marriage from the beginning," she said slowly.

Anthony turned around in surprise. He had not heard this before.

"Your mother should never have married your father," she said.

"Why not?" Anthony asked defensively as he moved back to his chair. "He was a good man."

Lady Elinor nodded in agreement. "Yes, he was, and he loved your mother, I'm sure of that." She stopped for a moment, looking down at her hands while she thought of her daughter. "The failure of their marriage was all your mother's fault. She lived in a dream world, where real love between a man and a woman did not have any place. When you talked about 'living happily ever after,' you unconsciously chose your words very well. That was exactly what she thought. She imagined her life would be one party after another. Any children would be tucked away in the nursery, cared for by others. She envisioned no pain, no hard times."

"Few people do at the beginning of a marriage," Anthony pointed out gently, seeing her distress.

Lady Elinor looked up at him and shook her head sadly. "But she envisioned no sharing and no compromising, either. She closed herself off from the real joy of marriage because she could not really join with your father in building a life together. What she thought was love died very quickly once it was faced with reality."

"You are very sure that it wasn't really love," Anthony said dryly.

"Of course it wasn't," Lady Elinor said, recovering some of her usual briskness. "Real love doesn't die when it comes face to face with real life. It can cause you great happiness or terrible pain, but it doesn't float away because the one you love doesn't always speak in flowery phrases, and even occasionally mentions things like toothaches or dirty laundry."

Anthony could not resist a small smile. "Is that what father dared to mention?" he asked.

Lady Elinor nodded. "That and more, I fear. You saw how unhappy they both were. That's why I want you to wait for the right person. You mustn't be caught in that same trap."

Anthony stood up and smoothed his coat down. "You seem to be forgetting the fact that I am already betrothed, and that I am certain I have found the right person. But even if I haven't, it is too late to do anything about it except graciously accept my choice."

"That is a lot of faradiddle," Lady Elinor snorted rudely. "Other men have broken off engagements, and yours hasn't even been announced."

"Perhaps a few other men have behaved so dishonorably," he conceded, "but I could never expose Blanche to such public ridicule, and my family to the scandal that would surely follow. However, all that is immaterial. I have given my word to Blanche and shall keep it, not because I fear being ostracized by society, but because I want to marry her."

He turned and began to walk toward the door, missing the look of disgust that his grandmother gave him. As he opened the door his grandmother called him back.

"I almost forgot," she said, smiling at him. "I wanted you to escort us to the theatre Wednesday night."

Anthony looked put out, and was quickly seeking a reason to refuse.

"You did promise to take us where we wanted to go," she reminded him innocently. She could see that he was wavering, and went on to add, "Perhaps after the theatre, we could discuss that invitation to Blanche."

Anthony gritted his teeth. "I'll make the arrangements," he said ungraciously, then stomped from the room.

CHAPTER SEVEN

Stacy, who had never imagined anything like the "Drury Lane" Theatre, stared about her in wonder at the theatre itself and all the people milling about inside. Just when she thought that nothing could be more exciting, the curtains were pulled aside and the show began.

Anthony found the performance of *As You Like It* mediocre at best and was hard put not to fall asleep, but at the intermission Stacy and Laurie cried out and clapped as if they were seeing Edmund Kean himself. Anthony tried to sink lower in his chair, thankful that Blanche had had other plans for the evening.

"Wasn't that exciting?" Stacy sighed in awe.

"Terribly," Anthony said sarcastically, trying to stifle a yawn.

Stacy made a face at him and turned to Lady Elinor. In doing so, the beads on her reticule caught on the fringe of her shawl. She stood up, trying to free it, but it was quite firmly entangled. Finally, in desperation, she gave a hard tug. The sound of beads showering onto the floor could be heard even in the neighboring boxes.

"Oh, dear," Stacy cried faintly.

A vast understatement, Anthony thought as he leaned forward to help retrieve the beads. Laurie was already scrambling on the floor picking them up, so Anthony took Stacy's arm and moved her, none too gently, out of the way.

"I'm sorry," she muttered uncertainly.

Anthony ignored her, but Laurie gave her an encouraging grin. In a few minutes he stood up again.

"I think I have them all," he said as he emptied his hands into the lining of her purse.

"It doesn't matter if you don't," she assured him.

"It will if we fall on them," Anthony pointed out cynically.

Stacy blushed, but Lady Elinor winked at her. "Anthony just isn't used to the theatre being quite this exciting," she said.

Anthony sent her a black look as they heard voices approaching their box, and Jeremy Chetwin put his head in. "Are we welcome?" he asked.

He pulled aside the curtain to let Cecilia and her grandmother enter, but once that courtesy was done, he hurried over to Stacy's side.

"Have you enjoyed the play?" he asked her.

Stacy stole a look at Anthony and was surprised to see his lips twitching. "Oh, yes," she said to Jeremy. "It is just wonderful here." She tried to turn to Cecilia, but Jeremy seemed determined to hold her attention.

"You are looking particularly lovely tonight," he said to her.

Stacy thanked him quickly, but her attention was on Cecilia, whom she knew was conscious of Jeremy's every move. She looked about her quickly, seeking a way to force him back to Cecilia's side.

"I certainly would like a lemonade," Laurie said suddenly, and stood up. "Could I get something for anyone else?"

Stacy seized the opportunity with delight. "Oh, yes, I would like something, and I'm sure that the other ladies would, too." She smiled at Jeremy. "Why don't you go with him to help?" she suggested innocently.

Jeremy could hardly refuse, although he made it plain that he did not like leaving her side. He and Laurie left the box, and Stacy moved closer to Cecilia.

"Have you known Mr. Chetwin very long?" she asked the other girl.

"Oh, yes," Cecilia sighed. "Our country homes are very close. I have known Jeremy and Blanche since I was very young."

"Then you and Blanche are friends also?" Stacy asked hesitantly.

Cecilia wrinkled her nose expressively. "I wouldn't say friends, really," she said. "Up to a few months ago she didn't pay much attention to me. Then she began to take an interest in everything I do."

"I'm not sure I'd like that," Stacy said.

Cecilia shrugged. "She's so organized that she frightens me. I can never remember anything when I'm with her. She must think I have no opinions at all."

Laurie and Jeremy returned carrying the glasses of lemonade. Although there were several empty chairs in the box, it seemed clear to Stacy that Jeremy intended to take the one next to her and to exclude Cecilia once more.

Rather than give him that chance, Stacy got up quickly and sat down on the other side of Anthony. "How are your horses?" she asked him, giving him her full attention.

Anthony had been gazing absently into the crowd below them. "What?" he said, turning to stare at her in surprise.

"Your horses," she repeated impatiently, glancing briefly at Jeremy. With a shudder she pictured him carrying her chair around Anthony so he could sit beside her. She turned, giving Anthony her full attention, hoping Jeremy would think she was too engrossed in conversation to disturb.

"They are fine, I imagine," Anthony said, his glance following hers. Jeremy was frowning at her and looking hurt. He sat down next to Cecilia ungraciously and watched Stacy moodily.

"Do you ride much while staying in the city?" Stacy asked Anthony quickly, ignoring Jeremy's pout.

"Not as often as I'd like," Anthony said, realizing her purpose with surprise. The women of his acquaintance usually tried to gather as many men as possible around them, regardless of any other woman's feelings. He smiled at her warmly, allowing her loveliness to charm him. "You must miss riding, since you used to do it so often. Would you like to go riding with me tomorrow?" he asked.

Stacy was surprised by the offer and answered quickly, before he could change his mind. "I would love to, but I don't have a horse here in town."

"That's no problem." He shook his head with a laugh. "I'm sure that I can find a horse for you."

Stacy's excitement knew no bounds. "Oh, that's marvelous," she cried, clapping her hands. "I wish it were tomorrow already."

Anthony had to laugh again, noting with some surprise how lovely she was when she laughed.

Jeremy had noticed her excitement too. "I think we had better go back to our box," he said, his voice surly. Mrs. Frayne and Cecilia said their good-byes and went out into the hall. Jeremy followed, after giving Anthony and Stacy an angry glare.

"I think you may have lost an ardent admirer," Anthony whispered to Stacy as he left the box.

But Stacy just shrugged. "What is an ardent admirer compared to a horse, anyway?" she laughed.

"You will come in for a little while, won't you?" Lady Elinor asked Anthony as the carriage slowed to a stop in front of her house. She had noticed that he and Stacy had been cordial to one another, and hoped to push them together even more.

"Perhaps for a few minutes," Anthony said. He jumped out of the carriage, and helped his grandmother and then Stacy out. It was still early, and he was not particularly anxious to get home.

Since Lady Elinor took Laurie's arm, Anthony offered his to Stacy. She took it without thinking, happily talking about the prospect of riding again soon. A group of men walked by them; one rather portly man nodded to Anthony and took a long look at Stacy. Anthony felt her shrink back against his arm, and laughed quietly as they entered the house.

"He's perfectly harmless," he told her quietly. "I've known Hugo Palmer for years."

She said nothing, but let go of his arm as they entered the sitting room.

"Help yourself to a drink," Lady Elinor told Anthony. "I think I could use some tea." She watched Anthony walk over to the liquor cabinet and noticed Stacy standing by herself near the door. "Laurie, come with me and help," she ordered, as if she had no staff to prepare the tea. She bustled out, expecting him to follow her.

As soon as the door had closed behind her, Laurie rushed over to Stacy's side. "What's wrong?" he asked in concern.

Anthony, who had been pouring himself a glass of brandy, turned around at Laurie's question. Stacy was as white as a sheet and trembling. He put his glass down and walked across the room toward her.

Laurie had led her to a chair and was stooped down by her, holding her hand. Anthony stopped a few feet away.

"What's the matter?" Laurie asked her again.

Stacy looked at him, her eyes wide with fear. "It's Mr. Palmer," she said in a hoarse whisper.

"Oh, is that all?" Anthony turned to Laurie impatiently. "He is an acquaintance of mine who passed us coming into the house. He was not the slightest bit rude, in spite of what her appearance might lead you to suspect." He looked at her frightened expression and shook his head in disgust. Then he walked back to finish pouring his brandy. Anyone who took fright that easily shouldn't be allowed out in the world, he thought irritably.

But Laurie did not dismiss the matter so quickly. "Did he see you?" he asked her.

She nodded, tears overflowing her eyes and running down her cheeks.

"Laurie!" his grandmother called from down the hall. How could the romance flourish if he was in there? "Laurie, come here!" she called.

"Blast!" Laurie muttered, glancing at the door.

"Just what is all the fuss about?" Anthony asked impatiently. He had poured his drink, only to return to find the troublesome chit crying.

"Laurie!" Lady Elinor was becoming impatient.

"What am I going to do?" Stacy cried, clinging to Laurie's hands desperately.

Laurie glanced at the door and then up at his brother, frowning at them both. "Tell Anthony," he decided quickly.

Stacy stared at him in disbelief, but he just shook his head. "I don't know how to help you anymore," he said, "but Anthony will."

"Laurie!" His grandmother sounded quite angry and very close.

Laurie jumped to his feet and let go of Stacy's hand. "He's really not so bad," he consoled her, then left the room.

Stacy stared down at her hands for what seemed like years, while Anthony stood there waiting. When it appeared that she was not going to volunteer any information, he sat down heavily next to her and sighed.

"Why are you afraid of Hugo Palmer?" he asked.

Stacy still did not look up, but twisted her hands nervously in her lap. "He's the one Mr. Barlowe had arranged for me to marry," she said quietly.

Anthony snorted in disbelief. "He's already married and has a houseful of children."

Stacy did look up then. "No," she said, shaking her head, "his wife died last year, leaving him with a houseful of girls. He was hoping that I could do better."

Anthony stared at her for a moment. He did not know whether to be outraged at the very idea or to laugh at its ridiculousness. "He's old enough to be your father," Anthony pointed out.

Stacy nodded, her eyes filling up with tears once more. *Good Lord,* Anthony thought, *she's telling the truth.* He sat dumbly watching the tears roll down her face, then reached over and pulled her into his arms.

She leaned against him, quietly crying into his coat. "So that's why you and Laurie eloped," he said, suddenly seeing the reason behind it.

Stacy nodded in his arms. "It seemed like the only solution."

"The only solution!" Anthony cried in hurt tones,

conveniently forgetting his earlier animosity toward her. "Why didn't you come to me for help?"

Stacy pulled away from him in surprise. "You would barely speak to me," she reminded him. "All I had was Laurie."

He reflected on that in dejected silence for a moment, then she put her hand softly on his arm. "What will happen now?" she asked him. "Can Mr. Barlowe still make me marry him?"

"Of course not," Anthony declared, angry at the very idea. "You're engaged to me now, remember?"

Stacy blushed and looked down at her hands. "But what if he finds out it isn't real?" she asked. "What can he do?"

"He won't find out," Anthony assured her, "and even if he does, I won't let you marry somebody like Palmer. When you marry, it'll be the person you want, I promise you."

Stacy smiled up in relief. Her eyes were still watery, but her tears seemed to magnify their loveliness. Anthony suddenly caught his breath as he looked down at her. She was so lovely and so close . . .

He bent his head, and softly, gently, his lips touched hers. She drew back slightly, startled, but his arms slid around her, and she seemed to realize how perfectly she fit there.

Her lips were as soft as rose petals and like a drug, for Anthony felt he could not get enough of them. He kissed her again and again, until her arms crept around his neck and she was kissing him back.

His hands slid along her back, pressing her closer to him, molding her body to the shape of his. He did not remember anyone else. The only thing of importance was the perfect way they seemed to blend together. It was more than their bodies; their spirits, too, seemed to be clinging together.

Suddenly the perfection was gone. Stacy was pushing him away from her and staring at him in horror. Anthony stared back, trying to comprehend the fact that it had been Stacy who had aroused such passion in him.

With sudden decisiveness, Anthony lifted Stacy off his lap, strode over to the brandy, and poured himself another glass. "I don't know what to say," he mumbled into it. "I hope you can forgive me."

She turned away from him slowly, her eyes on the carpet, and wrapped her arms around herself tightly. She was trembling violently from the emotions he had caused in her—emotions she had never before experienced.

"I thought I'd never get away," Laurie laughed as he hurried back into the room. He looked from Stacy to Anthony. "Did you get everything settled?"

Stacy nodded dumbly, afraid to speak for fear of crying again, while Anthony said, "No, we hadn't finished yet."

Laurie's forehead creased in confusion as he

turned from one to the other. "Did I interrupt something?" he asked uncertainly.

"Yes," Anthony cried, but Stacy said, "No."

Anthony looked at Stacy's back, wishing that his brother would quietly disappear for a few minutes.

"I'm bringing the tea along," Lady Elinor called from the hallway. Her footsteps could be heard coming closer and closer.

"Blast!" Anthony cried in frustration. "Why doesn't the whole house join us here?" He quickly emptied his glass and put it down angrily. After nodding to his brother he rushed out of the room.

"He was certainly in a hurry," Laurie exclaimed with a laugh as he watched the door swing closed. He turned back to Stacy as it opened again to admit Lady Elinor and a footman carrying the tea. "Was he able to help?"

Stacy looked at him and, feeling utterly stupid, burst into tears again. "Not now," she pleaded and, pushing past Lady Elinor in the doorway, ran up to her room.

CHAPTER EIGHT

Laurie presented himself at the Johnson house in the early afternoon. He had been so excited about the prospect of seeing Althea again that he had hardly eaten that day and had spent more than an hour dressing carefully.

He had never tried to follow the latest fashions, and knew that his coat was not the newest cut, but he had sneaked into Anthony's room and borrowed one of his snowy white cravats. After three attempts that only rumpled it slightly, Laurie felt that he had achieved a close copy of the "Orientale," one of Anthony's favorite styles.

A grim-faced lady opened the door and showed him into the parlor, where Althea was waiting for him. She did not appear to be aware of his arrival but was seated near a window, staring out, a book lying forgotten in her lap.

Laurie watched her for a moment, lost in appreciation of the lovely picture she so unconsciously presented. She was wearing a pink muslin dress that was trimmed with ruffles along the neck, the sleeves, and the hem. Amid the ruffles, tiny pink bows were hidden. Her beautiful blond hair was pulled back from her face and fell into soft curls that rested on her shoulders. A narrow pink ribbon was woven through the curls and tied into a bow at the back of her head. She was all innocence and beauty.

Laurie sighed, and Althea turned sharply. "Why Mr. Kendall," she cried, rising to her feet. Her right hand rested lightly over her heart, betraying the fact that he had startled her. "I had no idea you had arrived," she apologized softly, her long dark lashes fluttering down so that Laurie was deprived the joy of gazing into her wonderful blue eyes.

"Won't you be seated?" she suggested, her left hand gracefully indicating a chair near hers.

Laurie moved over to the chair awkwardly, feeling large and clumsy next to such fragile beauty. He sat nervously on the edge of his chair.

Althea gazed over at him with a shy smile, then lowered her eyes to her hands, which were resting in her lap. "I was so terribly embarrassed that my brother bothered you," she told him. "It is such an imposition, and he had no right to ask it of you."

"Oh, no," Laurie protested. "I was honored that he felt he could entrust you to my care."

She gazed up at him again, and Laurie felt himself blushing. She appeared not to notice his suddenly red face, and smiled gratefully. "You are so kind," she sighed in relief. "I did not want my company forced on you."

Laurie slid forward even farther on his chair. Balancing precariously on the edge, he hastened to assure her, "I am yours to command. Just tell me where you would like to go today. It will be my privilege to escort you there."

"Well, I did have some shopping to do," she admitted hesitantly, "but I'm sure that you must have things you would prefer doing to following me about Pantheon's Bazaar while I shop."

Laurie assured her once more that there was nothing he had to do that in any way compared to the honor of being her companion, and at last she seemed satisfied. She allowed him to hire a carriage, and soon, accompanied by her maid, they were wandering among the treasures at the bazaar.

Laurie had never been shopping with a young lady before, for Stacy never did much of that sort of thing. He was amazed at how much time it took to decide between two pairs of gloves, when they both looked the same to him. He was not impatient, though, for while Althea chose her gloves he was allowed the luxury of gazing adoringly at her.

Once the gloves were chosen, and Laurie had begged for and received the privilege of carrying them, they moved to the area that sold lengths of fabric. Laurie saw nothing to be excited about there, but Althea went into transports of delight.

"There are so many things that I need," she told him confidentially, "and Thomas wants me to make some new dresses for myself. I fear that he feels the ones I have are rather shabby."

"Oh, no." Laurie shook his head in protest. "I'm sure that you would look lovely no matter what you wore."

He blushed again when she smiled at him, then she began to walk among the tables. She selected lengths of muslin, satin, and velvet, each in several different colors, and piled them rapidly into her maid's waiting arms. Laces, ribbons, and beaded trims were tossed on the top, then buttons and threads.

Laurie watched in surprise at how quickly she seemed to choose. There was none of the indecision that she had shown over the gloves. The pile was growing quite large, and at a rapid rate.

At last Althea seemed to have run out of things to select, and the saleslady helping her began to add up her total. Laurie glanced aimlessly around the room, while Althea discussed her purchases with her maid. When the clerk finished her figuring, Althea reached for her reticule. Her cry of dismay brought Laurie to her side immediately.

"What's wrong?" he cried, seeing her distress.

"My money is gone," she whispered to Laurie in despair. "I had quite a few notes left when I bought the gloves, but they are gone." She looked around her nervously, moving closer to Laurie for protection, while the maid twisted her hands in fear. "Someone must have stolen them."

Laurie looked up and saw the saleslady watching them suspiciously. "Is there some problem?" she asked acidly.

"No," Laurie said quickly, knowing that he had failed to protect Althea as he had promised. What would her brother think? Would he ever trust him with her again?

Deciding quickly, Laurie reached for his own money, hoping he had enough. He asked for the total, and was relieved to see that he did indeed have enough money, but just barely. He paid the woman and gathered Althea's bundles together.

"If you hadn't been there to help me, it would have been awful." Althea's slight body shuddered expressively. "The people looked at me so suspiciously. Thank God I wasn't alone," Althea said in relief. She put her hand gently on Laurie's arm and gazed up into his face, her eyes reflecting her gratitude. "I'll make sure that you get all your money back," she promised him. "Thomas will repay you."

Laurie shook his head quickly. "No, please," he said. "Let's not tell him."

"But . . ." Althea was astonished.

"It was all my fault," Laurie cried in anguish, interrupting her. "If I had been watching the people around you better, it would never have happened. No one would have had the chance to rob you." He swallowed nervously. "Your brother will think I'm irresponsible, and he'll never trust me with you again."

Althea was silent for a moment after his passionate outburst. "I don't think it's right for you to pay," she said hesitantly, her face looking downward, hiding a secret smile. "But I understand your feelings." She looked up at him shyly. "I, too, would hate for Thomas to keep us apart."

Laurie breathed a sigh of relief as he and the maid picked up her bundles and they walked from the store. Once out in the street, Laurie waved down a hackney.

Before it reached them, a frantic voice called out behind them. "Miss Johnson," they heard. "Miss Johnson!"

Laurie started to turn around as the carriage stopped in front of them. Putting a restraining hand on Laurie's arm, Althea said, "We had better take this carriage or someone else will."

They heard her name called again, closer this time, and Laurie turned to see a young man hurrying toward them. He looked to be about Laurie's age and was dressed neatly in obviously expensive clothes.

"Hello, Miss Johnson," he greeted Althea enthusiastically.

She reluctantly turned around and nodded at him. "Hello, Mr. Lipton," she said nervously. "What a surprise, seeing you here." Her voice sounded anything but overjoyed.

Laurie wondered if this young man was one of those he was supposed to protect Althea against, but he seemed harmless. He was just staring at her adoringly, his face an alarming shade of red.

"Do ya want this hack er not?" the coachman broke in rudely.

"Of course, we do," Althea said sharply, nudging Laurie into action. He quickly loaded the bundles inside, while she smiled at the young man. "It was so nice to see you again," she said softly. Her smile caused him to stammer incoherently, and before he could speak, Laurie had assisted her and her maid into the coach.

As they pulled away, Laurie could see the young man gazing after them, still wearing the same bemused expression.

"Is he a friend of yours?" Laurie asked, turning to Althea.

She shrugged expressively. "One meets so many people," she said, her voice drifting off as if the matter were of little importance. Then she turned her lovely gaze on Laurie and dazzled him with a smile. "You will stay for some tea, won't you?" she asked, her eyes imploring him to agree.

Stacy was horribly ashamed of her behavior. It was bad enough that she had actually confided in Anthony about Mr. Palmer, but then she had thrown herself at him. It was true that she had not meant for him to kiss her, but she had practically begged him to hold her in his arms, which was almost as bad.

She paced around her bedroom nervously, wracked with indecision. She desperately wanted to go riding, but she did not know how she could ever face Anthony again. He must be thoroughly disgusted with her.

Her cheeks burned with the thought of his kisses, and she put her hands up to try to wipe the color away. Even if that had been possible, her memory kept bringing back a vivid replay of their embrace, focusing on her enthusiastic response to his every touch.

How could she have acted that way with Anthony, of all people! she cried to herself, thinking of all the times she had vented her anger against him.

If only he had laughed at her or been furiously angry, Stacy moaned as she threw herself across her bed. Then, at least, she could have found relief in anger; but instead he had said nothing to her, leaving her to be consumed with shame.

She could almost see him standing there, watching her, and rising to her knees she angrily threw her pillow at the spot. "Get out of here, you horrible man!" she cried.

"Why, Miss Stacy!"

Stacy spun around to see her maid standing in the doorway, staring at her in wonder. Mary came a little farther into the room, closing the door behind her, and looked at the pillow in the middle of the floor.

Smiling sheepishly, Stacy climbed down off the bed and retrieved the pillow. As she walked across the room, Mary noticed her dress.

"Why, you aren't ready yet!" she cried. "Lord Kendall is here, and you don't even have your habit on." She continued to scold Stacy as she bustled about the room, trying to get her dressed.

"I don't think I'll go, after all," Stacy told her defiantly.

"Nonsense," Mary said, not pausing for a moment. She brushed Stacy's hair into a halo of curls, then quickly pulled her riding dress on. It was buttoned up, the jacket put on, and her bonnet was tied under her chin before Stacy had a chance to protest.

Well, she had to face Anthony sometime, Stacy thought fatalistically as she allowed herself to be rushed down the stairs. The sitting room door was opened for her, and she forced herself to enter.

Anthony had had a very restless night also, and he envisioned himself as the veriest blackguard. He kept remembering all the times in the past when Stacy had sworn hatred of him, and he forgot entirely that he had expressed equal dislike of her. Now she was the lovely young innocent he had taken advantage of, in spite of the fact that she despised him. He would not be surprised if she refused to speak to him ever again.

In spite of this guilt Anthony found himself unable to stay away from her. She held some mysterious fascination for him that grew each time he was with her. It was respect and friendship, he told himself, unwilling to probe his feelings more deeply.

He was willing to admit to himself that she was not the irresponsible child he had first thought, and he felt genuinely sorry for her, caught in circumstances as she was. But, he reminded himself, she was still very much a child, despite her age.

He had come to take Stacy riding with mixed feelings. He was afraid that his actions of the night before might cause her to regard him suspiciously, and that they would be back to their old antagonistic footing. Worse still was the fear that his grandmother might have learned what had happened and be taking his actions much more seriously. Instead of understanding it as a temporary aberration, she would be bound to believe it was indicative of stronger feelings on his part.

Apparently, Lady Elinor knew nothing of what had happened, for he received only a light scolding for not saying good-bye the night before. The subject was then dropped in favor of his alfresco party.

However, it was obvious when Stacy entered that she had not dismissed the previous night quite as easily. She came no farther into the room than just inside the door, and stood there twisting her hands together nervously. She favored him with quick glances that showed her eyes as deep pools of blue in her starkly white face.

Lady Elinor saw nothing strange in Stacy's behavior. She wished them a happy ride, then rushed them out of the house, smiling coyly all the while.

Anthony had chosen a lively brown mare for Stacy that should have had her screaming in delight, but now, because of his stupidity, she didn't even want to be near him.

The groom moved over to Stacy's side to help her mount, but Anthony waved him aside. He walked over to her and took her hand in his, but her eyes remained downward.

"I want to apologize for my behavior last night," he said hesitantly. Her eyes flew up to his in surprise as he went on. "I hope you can forgive me."

Stacy's forehead creased in puzzlement. "But I was the one who behaved badly," she said in a rush. "It was my unseemly display that brought on . . ." Her face blushed delightfully as she stammered.

"Then you weren't angry with me?" he asked in relief.

Stacy shook her head wordlessly, a smile playing about her lips. It suddenly broke through, making her eyes sparkle and her face glow. "I was afraid that I had ruined everything by my behavior," she laughed "and that you'd never want to be friends."

The idea of friendship between them did not seem so implausible to Anthony now as it might have at one time. In fact, it was almost disappointing. He tightened his hold on her hand as he gazed down into her laughing face. "Do you really think we can stop arguing?" he teased.

Stacy looked at the horse restlessly waiting at her side. "As long as I can ride this horse, I'll agree with you about anything," she laughed.

They mounted their horses and Anthony led the way to Green Park, where they would have more space to ride. He had planned on challenging her to race, but he found that it was very difficult to take his eyes from her lovely face, so they rode side by side. The groom rode a short distance behind them.

"Have you named your foal yet?" Stacy asked as they brought their horses to a halt at the top of a hill.

Anthony forced himself out of the daze he was in, and tried to focus on her question. "Uh, no," he said hesitantly, then laughed. "The poor thing is almost two months old, so I had better decide on one."

Stacy leaned across her horse toward him. "Actually, I found the perfect name for him," she said.

"Oh?" he said skeptically.

Stacy frowned at him in mock displeasure. "Don't look so doubtful," she scolded. "I have had some very good ideas in the past."

As soon as she said that, she thought of quite a few that did not fall into that category, but Anthony was polite enough not to contradict her. "Well, let's hear this one," he said, pretending indifference.

"I thought the perfect name for Moonlight's foal would be Pegasus," Stacy told him excitedly. "It's the name of a constellation," she added.

"Pegasus," he murmured, trying out the name. "Yes, I like it," he said, wondering why he had never noticed before how her eyes sparkled when she was excited.

"Remember the book you carried in the library for me?" she asked. "I found it in there."

"That's what you had me carry that tome for?" he asked, shaking his head. "I suppose I shouldn't complain, since you were doing it for me, but my arms still ache from the weight of it."

Stacy looked horrified. "Oh, I'm so sorry," she cried, her eyes wide with fear. "I hadn't realized it at the time just how old and weak you are."

"You wretch!" Anthony cried, and reached out for her arm, but she evaded him, and with a wild peal of laughter she kicked her horse and galloped down the hill.

Anthony took off after her. She had quite a good lead, but his horse was larger, and he caught up with her as they passed through a grove of trees. He managed to get hold of her reins and pull her horse to a stop. She slid to the ground, laughing and out of breath.

"Why, you little devil!" Anthony said softly as he dismounted and walked around his horse toward her. "You're going to pay for that remark."

Stacy giggled and watched him gleefully. As he got closer to her, she slipped under her horse's reins and out of his reach.

"You can't run away," he teased, waving her horse's reins in the air. "I've still got these, and it's a long walk home. You'll have to apologize."

She shook her head with a grin and ducked out of his way again. "I'll just find some younger man who'll come to my rescue."

"I have you now," he said, making a quick grab for her arm. She darted away too slowly, and he pulled her closer to him. "Are you going to take back all those nasty remarks?" he threatened her fiercely.

She shook her head quickly, trying not to laugh. "Never!"

Stacy's horse moved slightly, pushing her closer to Anthony. Their laughter died suddenly as Anthony gazed down into Stacy's eyes. The whole world seemed to stand still as his head bent slowly toward hers until their lips met.

There was no hesitation on Stacy's part this time. Her arms slid up around his neck, pulling him closer, while his hands moved across her back. She responded completely to him, blindly letting him arouse feelings in her that she had never known existed.

His lips left hers, trailing slowly down her neck, and she shivered in delight. His lips found their way back to hers, his hold tightening as his kiss deepened.

They gave no thought to their surroundings but just lost themselves in the ecstasy of their embrace. Suddenly Stacy's horse snorted and moved away from her. The movement caused her to lose her balance slightly, and their hold was broken.

For a long moment they just stared at each other, neither sure of what had happened. The sound of the groom approaching on his horse broke the silence, and Stacy looked away from Anthony, biting her lip in consternation and fighting an almost overwhelming desire to cry. Since she had just been ecstatically happy a few seconds ago, it seemed a ridiculous way to feel.

"Maybe we ought to go," she mumbled to Anthony.

Nodding, he helped her onto her horse; then, after he had mounted his own, they rode home in silence.

CHAPTER NINE

The carriage came to a stop in front of Kenwood, and Jeremy jumped out. Scraping an elaborate bow, he held up his hand. "Allow me, lovely lady," he said to a giggling Cecilia. She took his hand and, blushing brightly, allowed him to help her down. Stacy watched with a smile.

The ride had started out quietly enough, with Cecilia locked in her shell of shyness and Jeremy flirting outrageously with Stacy. She had refused to take him seriously, though, and had laughed outright at his ridiculous compliments. Soon Laurie and Cecilia had joined in the teasing as well.

Jeremy had taken it all very good-naturedly, and had begun to include Cecilia in his attentions. She had not seemed to mind that his flattery was all in fun. By the end of the ride Cecilia's cheeks were flushed and her eyes sparkling. Stacy thought it was not only the laughter that had caused her glowing appearance, but also Jeremy's attention. She only hoped that the others had noticed how attractive Cecilia was looking.

Jeremy offered his arm to Cecilia as they waited for Laurie and Stacy to get out of the carriage. "How nice that you have finally arrived," a slightly scolding voice reached them from the top of the stairs.

They turned as a group to see Blanche smiling a cold greeting down at them.

"Thinks she lives here already," Laurie mumbled resentfully. Raising his voice slightly, he said, "I was just welcoming them to my home."

Blanche's eyebrows raised slightly at his belligerent tone, but she said nothing, turning instead to Cecilia and her brother. "Cecilia, my dear, how lovely you look today!" She spoke in condescending tones, as if she were talking to a dim-witted child. "You must be careful today, Jeremy, or someone will steal her away from you."

Jeremy dropped Cecilia's arm and moved away from her slightly, while he glared at Blanche. His sister appeared not to notice, and came down the stairs to Cecilia's side. "I have found just the pattern for those chair covers I suggested you make," she told her quietly. "One day next week we must shop for the silks."

Cecilia nodded halfheartedly, while Stacy fumed for her friend. She was about to say something rude to Blanche when Anthony hurried out of the house to greet them, a sincere smile of welcome on his face. "We thought you were lost," he laughed, unaware of the tension in the air. He spoke to all of them, but his eyes sought out Stacy. Suddenly shy, she blushed and looked downward.

"The rest of the guests are on the terrace and the south lawn," Anthony said. "Why don't we join them?"

Stacy felt someone take her arm, and looked up in surprise to see Jeremy next to her. He led her across the lawn to where they could see others standing. Stacy looked back quickly. Cecilia and Laurie were following Anthony and Blanche inside.

"That was terribly rude," Stacy scolded him. She stopped walking and pulled her arm away from him. "How can you be so insensitive to Cecilia?"

Jeremy looked like a sulking little boy. "Oh, bother Cecilia!" he said, kicking at the grass with his boot.

"I thought you liked her," Stacy said in exasperation.

Jeremy glanced up at her, shrugging his shoulders. "I used to," he admitted reluctantly, "but she's turned into a mouse lately."

"She thinks very much of you," Stacy pointed out. He said nothing, but shifted his feet uncomfortably. "You probably hurt her feelings by walking off with me."

"Oh, no," Jeremy shook his head. "I'm sure by now Blanche has thought up some excuse for my behavior, and the two of them are busy making plans. Or rather," he corrected himself bitterly, "Blanche is making plans while Cecilia nods her head."

Stacy looked at him in bewilderment. "I don't understand what you mean," she said slowly.

Jeremy smiled suddenly, an infectious grin that Stacy found hard to resist. He reached over and took her hand. "Never mind about them," he said offhandedly. "I've had a much better thought. Why don't we get married?"

Stacy stared at him for a moment, totally stunned by his suggestion. "You can't be serious!" she stammered.

"We'd have a marvelous time," he said, warming up to the idea. "And Blanche would have a fit!"

"And poor Cecilia would be crushed!" Stacy pointed out harshly, grabbing back her hand.

"That's not my fault," Jeremy said, losing some of his enthusiasm. "Blanche is the one who has led her to believe I care about her. Doesn't it matter who I care about?"

"I am not sure that you know who you care

140

about," she told him. "You seem to flit about to whatever girl is present. I don't believe for one minute that your proposal was based on love. It sounds more like a desire to irritate Blanche."

Jeremy looked ill at ease for a moment, but he admitted nothing. "I do love you," he insisted stubbornly. "And I will find a way to prove it to you."

He tried to take her hand again, but as she stepped back to avoid him they heard voices approaching. Stacy spun around and saw that the others had left the house and were crossing the lawn to the party. She was not aware of Anthony's eyes following her, but she saw the hurt in Cecilia's.

Stacy moved away from Jeremy quickly, and silently vowed to stay as far from him as possible. She joined Laurie, taking his arm and smiling up at him. She was vaguely aware of Jeremy reluctantly joining his sister and Cecilia, but she refused even to glance in his direction.

Staying away from Jeremy proved to be a time-consuming task, for he seemed determined to be with Stacy. She drifted from group to group, chatting happily and smiling incessantly, but was aware of his constant presence. She thought that if she stayed close to Laurie all her problems would be solved, but he was inattentive and tended to wander away.

Stacy was ready to cry in frustration. She had looked forward to this party with great anticipation.

She had expected it to be so wonderful to be back in the country again, but now she couldn't even relax and enjoy it. She had to spend all her time dodging Jeremy and trying to stay close to Laurie. It kept her so busy that she had no time to be nervous about seeing Anthony again, which perhaps was best, she decided suddenly.

"Laurie," she called impatiently. He had wandered away again, and she hurried after him. "What is the matter with you today?"

Laurie looked startled that she had noticed. "Could we go somewhere and talk?" he blurted out.

Stacy looked around them. A buffet had been set up, and, having filled their plates, the guests were sitting around the grounds eating. A few were engaged in a croquet game a little way down the lawn. No one seemed to be paying any attention to them. Even Jeremy seemed to have deserted her, and was sitting with Anthony, Blanche, and Cecilia.

"Why don't we walk toward the stables?" she suggested.

Laurie took her arm, and they walked in silence. Stacy wondered what was distracting him so, but he made no attempt to talk until they were in the shade of the building.

"Oh, Stacy, the most wonderful thing has happened," Laurie told her, barely able to control his excitement. "I have fallen in love!"

This was not what Stacy had expected him to say,

and she stared at him for a moment in silence. "Who is she?" she asked finally. "Do I know her?"

Laurie mistook Stacy's surprised silence and looked at her with concern, fearing that he had hurt her unbearably. "After all, you did say you didn't want to marry me," he reminded her uncertainly.

Stacy burst into laughter and walked over to him. She slipped her arm through his and hugged it. "Oh, Laurie, you are a darling." Standing on her toes, she reached up and kissed his cheek, laughing again at his miserable look. "I am delighted that you have found someone. You just surprised me, that's all. And I wish you would stop worrying about me. I'm not going to change my mind and force you to marry me. Besides," she teased, "I'm engaged to Anthony now."

Laurie missed the humor she intended. "I'd much rather have you for a sister than Blanche," he said seriously. "It's too bad you hate each other so."

Stacy nodded, hoping that he would not expand that topic. She did not know what her feelings toward Anthony were, but she was sure that hate was no longer one of them. "Tell me about this girl. What is her name?" she asked eagerly, to distract him. "Do I know her?"

Laurie put his arm around her shoulders and led her around the end of the stables, where the horses could be seen in their pastures.

"I don't know why you had to invite her," Blanche whispered to Anthony as her eyes followed Stacy. They were sitting at a gaily decorated table under an old oak tree, their plates full of delectable treats, but Blanche was not tempted by them and pushed them about impatiently on her plate. She watched the guests enjoying their meal, and although the bright colors of the women's dresses made a delightful picture against the background of Anthony's garden, that did not please her either.

Anthony was watching Stacy, too, but not in Blanche's critical way. "How could I not invite her?" he asked. "She's staying with my grandmother. It would have been quite a slight if I had left her out."

"Your grandmother left me out," Blanche noted stiffly.

Anthony reluctantly took his eyes off Stacy and turned to the woman at his side. How was it that he had never noticed how dictatorial she was?

"I am hardly responsible for my grandmother's actions," he told her curtly. "Nor must I avenge every imagined slight by being intentionally rude."

Blanche stared at him in surprise, hardly believing that he had spoken to her that way. Before she could demand an apology, he was bowing stiffly and walking away. *Well, let him go,* she fumed, and turned to Cecilia and Jeremy, who had come to join them.

Anthony walked among his guests, chatting quietly and smiling but conscious only of the desire to get away from Blanche. Then he noticed Stacy and Laurie walking toward the stables, and thought that maybe he would join them. They, at least, were not always scolding him for something.

At the thought of being with Stacy, he began to walk a little faster. *How completely I misjudged her,* he said to himself. She was such a lively little thing, so delightful to be with. He didn't even mind her scolding, which she never hesitated to do. He shook his head with a laugh as he remembered how fiercely she would tear into him for the slightest reason.

Anthony rounded the corner of the house, and suddenly stopped short under the cover of some apple trees. There, by the stables, were Stacy and Laurie. She was holding his arm, and, as Anthony watched in horror, she leaned over and kissed his cheek.

Anthony felt a sudden rush of anger so frighteningly intense that he wanted to rush over to his brother and push him out of the way, crush him completely and gather Stacy into his own arms, where no other man might touch her.

As suddenly as the anger came, it went, leaving Anthony feeling cold and horrified. That was his brother, whom he loved; how could he be so jealous of him?

An icy claw seemed to settle around Anthony's heart as he watched Laurie put his arm around Stacy and lead her around the side of the stable. He tried to force down the realization that was pushing its way into his thoughts.

At some point in the last few weeks he had stopped fighting the attraction he felt toward Stacy and had allowed himself to fall hopelessly in love with her. And hopeless it truly was, for it was obvious from what he had just seen that she and Laurie loved each other. All he could ever hope to be to her was a brother. The revulsion that coursed through his body at the thought was unbelievably strong. He took a deep breath and willed himself to put Stacy from his mind. He loved Laurie too much ever to try to come between them. He shook his head as if to clear his thoughts, then turned back to join the others.

Anthony retraced his steps and came upon Blanche, Cecilia, Jeremy, and a few of the other guests on their way to the stables.

"We wanted to see your horses," Blanche explained with a smile.

Anthony graciously pointed out the way and let the others go ahead as Blanche came over and took his arm. "I'm sorry I was so silly before," she said under the cover of the general talking. "I never meant to anger you."

He nodded slowly, realizing that it was not Blanche who had suddenly become difficult, but himself. Understanding the reason for his change in behavior, he resolved to make it up to her. She was going to be his wife soon, and she deserved his loyalty and consideration.

"My grandmother delights in causing trouble, but I'll demand that she invite you soon," he promised.

Blanche's eyes sparkled. "Maybe she'll come to our ball, too," she suggested.

Anthony was saved from making any promises by the cries of admiration from the rest of the group. They had reached the meadow where Moonlight and her colt grazed.

"That's a beautiful colt," Jeremy said, coming out of his sulks. "He looks like he'll be a prime goer as he grows. Any plans for him?"

"He's not for sale, if that's what you're asking." Anthony laughed, noticing that Laurie and Stacy had joined them.

They watched the colt frolic for several minutes, while its mother walked slowly over to where they stood. She sniffed their hands and let them rub her nose, but soon went back across the grass.

"What have you named the colt?" Cecilia asked, turning to Anthony.

"I know what the perfect name would be," Blanche cried, before he had a chance to speak. He looked at her in surprise.

"Well, its mother is Moonlight, and he has that beautiful white star on his forehead," she explained to everyone, "so Star would be the perfect name for him." She smiled proudly at Anthony.

He forced himself to smile back at her, although he could feel Stacy watching him. He glanced over at her sadly, sensing her hurt bewilderment, then looked back at Blanche. "I think it's a marvelous name," he told her with a smile. "Star he shall be."

Holding Blanche's arm tightly, he turned and walked slowly back toward the house with her, leaving Stacy and Laurie behind.

Stacy did not know how she survived the rest of the party. She forced herself to smile brightly, and flirted with Mr. Granger or any other man that came near her. She was vaguely conscious of Laurie watching her, a worried frown on his face, but no one else seemed to sense that anything was wrong.

Certainly no one suspected how much she wanted to slip away and hide, and even she was not sure why. But when Anthony had chosen Blanche's name for the horse, it had hurt her almost more than she could bear. It was as if he had slapped her in the face and laughed at her.

Why should it matter? she asked herself angrily. Anthony had never been her friend, and even if he had been polite to her a few times in London, it was only because he was a gentleman. He was careful to be polite to everyone, even those he did not like. That she should be in that category brought tears to her eyes, so she determinedly looked around her.

"Mr. Granger," she called to him as he passed by, "you've hardly spoken to me all day."

He sat down eagerly at her side. "It's only because there was always such a crowd around you." He frowned at her sadly. "I had hoped to drive you down here in my carriage. Dare I hope that I might bring you home instead?"

"I'm sorry," Stacy said, shaking her head. "I've already made plans." She glanced away from him suddenly to discover Anthony watching her broodingly. She turned back to Mr. Granger. "We are going to Almacks tomorrow. Might we see you there?"

"If I may have the promise of a dance, I shall camp out on the doorstep and wait for your arrival," he said.

Stacy deliberately kept her eyes away from Anthony and missed the look of pain on his face as her laughter floated across to him. "Why, Mr. Granger, I should be delighted to dance with you, but only if you promise not to camp out there. I should hate to reserve a dance for someone who was not allowed in."

Mr. Granger laughed and, swooping down, lifted her hand to his lips. "You are a true delight," he declared, and kept her at his side until it was time for her to leave.

CHAPTER TEN

Jeremy came down the stairs quickly, humming quietly to himself. He stopped at the foot of the stairs to admire himself in an ornate, gold-framed mirror. He straightened his snow-white cravat and brushed a minute speck of lint from his deep red coat. He was looking his best and was quite aware of it.

Taking a last look, he turned to leave, and was startled to find his sister standing next to him. His appearance had not enchanted her into silent admiration, however, and, frowning severely, she remained steadfastly in his way.

"I want to talk to you, Jeremy," she informed him.

Jeremy glanced at the large clock hanging across

from the stairs. It was chiming the hour. "Not now," he protested breezily. "I have to hurry."

He tried to brush past her with a cheery smile, but she grabbed hold of his arm and pointed to the nearby drawing room. "Now," she said firmly.

Jeremy pouted and tried to loosen her grasp. "You don't need to crush the material to make your point," he protested.

She let go of him, but her expression did not change. Under her ferocious glare he turned and meekly entered the drawing room. She followed him, closing the door after her.

Jeremy stood in the middle of the room, impatiently waiting for the scolding to be finished so that he could leave. Blanche noted his impatience, and took her time settling herself into her chair and arranging her skirts.

"There is no need for the great rush you appear to be in," she informed him casually. "You aren't going anywhere."

"No?" His voice was sarcastic.

Blanche idly examined a simple bracelet she was wearing, turning it slightly so that the clasp was hidden from sight. "I have invited Mrs. Frayne and Cecilia over for tea today, and I expect you to be present."

"That's too bad." His tone was not sympathetic. "But since I did not issue the invitation, I fail to see why I must be here." He was becoming restless, but he forced himself to stand quietly and pretend indifference.

"You know very well why I expect you to be here," she replied, her anger obvious. "I didn't invite them here because I enjoy their company, but because it's time that you became more serious in your intentions."

"I agree," Jeremy said quietly. Blanche looked up in surprise. "I think that could very well be the problem." He spoke quietly, almost as if he were talking only to himself, and walked thoughtfully over to the window.

Blanche watched him suspiciously. "I was talking about your intentions toward Cecilia," she noted dryly.

Jeremy turned to look at her in astonishment. "But I have no intentions toward Cecilia," he said clearly. "If I had, surely I would have done something about them by now. I have known her for years. Why would I wait until she came to London to declare myself?"

Blanche's lips thinned angrily, even though she held a tight rein on her temper. "Then I can only suppose that your references are to Miss Prescott."

Jeremy nodded, noting with inner glee the sudden clenching of her fists. "And you're right. It's time that I declared myself."

Blanche stood up, clutching the back of her chair.

"Need I inform you that I find her totally unsuitable?"

Jeremy's lips twitched. "Unsuitable for what?" he asked innocently.

"To be your wife!" Blanche snapped. "She's just the type I'd expect you to choose!"

"And what is that supposed to mean?" Jeremy was angry now too, and he strode quickly across the room to stand in front of her.

Although Blanche was tall, her brother was taller, and, looking up at his grim features, she felt a moment's misgivings. "I don't believe she really cares for you," Blanche said.

Jeremy gave her a disgusted look and turned toward the door. "I can't see how that concerns you." He pulled the door open with a ruthless tug. "When I decide to marry, it'll be someone I choose, not some mouse you pick for me."

He marched through the door and stopped short. Standing in the hallway, directly behind the butler, were Mrs. Frayne and Cecilia. Although the older lady's face was carefully free of expression, Cecilia's white face clearly showed that they had heard enough of his argument with Blanche.

"Hello," he said weakly, shifting his feet uneasily.

"I was just about to knock," the butler informed him.

Jeremy nodded and stood aside from the doorway, showing them in with a wave of his hand. "Blanche told me that you were coming for tea." He tried to force a friendly tone in his voice, but no one smiled in response.

Dejectedly he followed the ladies into the drawing room and sat down, knowing that he could hardly leave now.

Blanche and Mrs. Frayne talked quietly about fashions while Cecilia listened, a determined smile on her face. A knock on the door interrupted them, and the tea tray was silently wheeled in. Blanche continued to talk as she poured the tea and passed the cups around.

Jeremy moved to a chair closer to the others and silently accepted his tea. He would have liked to join in the conversation, but he couldn't. He could not accuse anyone of excluding him; but he knew nothing about mentonnières, bavolets, or other bonnet trims. He drank his tea uneasily, certain that Blanche was deliberately trying to make him uncomfortable.

When the discussion changed from bonnets to the condition of all the plants in Mrs. Frayne's garden, Jeremy stood up and walked over to a window. He stared out absently, feeling rather abused. He had tried to make amends for his rudeness by staying for tea, but no one wanted him there anyway.

A gentle touch on his arm made him swing around in surprise. Cecilia was standing next to him. Jeremy glanced over at the others, but his sister and Mrs.

Frayne were still deep in discussion. He looked down questioningly at Cecilia.

"I wanted to say something to you," Cecilia said nervously. "We never seem to have a chance to talk, so I thought it ought to be now." She took a deep breath, turning for a moment to see if the others had noticed her absence. She glanced briefly at Jeremy, then turned to look out the window.

"I know that your sister hopes we will get married," she said quickly. "I would have had to be blind not to have noticed." She tried to laugh, but it came out shakily. "I can guess how you feel about having me forced on you."

Jeremy made a noise of disagreement, but, looking up at him, she shook her head. "No, I understand," she assured him. "And I can see why you like Stacy so much. She's very lovely." She pushed back a strand of her own straight brown hair, her eyes suspiciously bright.

Jeremy felt like a complete cad, but she was not trying to force him to contradict her, and she went on before he could deny her words. "I know that she doesn't always take you too seriously, but I thought maybe if I talked to her I could explain that there's nothing between us."

She looked up at Jeremy, waiting for his answer. "I feel awful," he mumbled.

Cecilia laughed quietly and patted his arm. "There's no reason to," she told him. "I never expected anything from you, despite what Blanche or my mother had in mind. I'm having a wonderful time in London, and I'd like to see you happy too." She smiled reassuringly at him, but he did not feel any better.

"Look, Jerry," she said firmly, unconsciously using his pet name. "When I marry, it will be to someone who loves me as much as I love him, not someone chosen by my mother." She softened her tone slightly. "If we were going to fall in love, don't you suppose we would have done so by now?"

Jeremy nodded his grudging agreement.

"So why mope?" she teased him, ignoring the pain her words were causing. "You must fight for the girl you love!"

He grinned down at her. "You're a real chum," he said and squeezed her hand. "I'll do just that, but if you would talk to her," he added hesitantly, "it might help."

Cecilia nodded with a smile. "I'll do it soon," she promised, then went back to her tea.

She was aware of Jeremy's eyes on her, but pretended to be engrossed in her grandmother's conversation. Out of the corner of her eye she saw him shrug his shoulders and leave the room. It was only as the door closed behind him and his footsteps died away that she allowed her smile to falter.

* * *

Stacy watched the dancers moving and swaying to the music, their rich apparel turning the ballroom into a flower garden of color. She sighed quietly and turned to the woman at her side.

"It's lovely, isn't it?" Lady Elinor asked her with a smile. "I've been here many times, but the magic of Almacks never fails to enchant me."

Stacy nodded silently, not revealing to her that her sigh had been caused by boredom. Her first visit had been so exciting, everything she had dreamed it would be, but this one was inexplicably flat. Even receiving permission to waltz had not helped.

She forced herself to smile at Jeremy, who was carrying a glass of orgeat toward her. He was certainly persistent in his attentions, she said to herself, and noticed with a frown that Cecilia was sitting across the room from them.

"Had you given up on me?" Jeremy laughed, handing her the glass.

Stacy took a careful sip and tried not to wince. She hated the drink but had not known how to discourage Jeremy from getting it for her.

"I see that Cecilia's here," she said casually, watching for some sign of interest but seeing none. "She's looking very lovely."

"Not anything like yourself, though, I'll wager," he said, an appreciative look in his eyes.

Stacy smiled at him and went back to watching the dancers. She knew her pale green dress was quite flattering and her hair was curled attractively, but it mattered little.

Mr. Granger came over to them. "The next dance is mine, I believe," he said, claiming her hand.

"No," Jeremy cried, quite offended. He turned to Stacy. "I thought the next one would be mine."

Stacy looked around nervously, afraid that his raised voice had caused attention. "No, it would cause talk if I were to sit with you and then dance with you," she pointed out to him quietly.

"What does that matter?" he cried. "Let them talk, let them all talk. Maybe their talk will make my dreams come true." He tried to pull her hand from Mr. Granger's grasp.

Stacy drew back from him, terribly embarrassed. She looked up at Mr. Granger, who understood her feelings and nodded toward the dance floor. "I believe that we should find our places in the set."

She allowed him to lead her to their place with relief. "I'm so sorry that happened," she said hesitantly.

But Mr. Granger only shrugged. "I can understand how he feels. I suffer the same agonies when I see you with another."

Stacy looked at him in astonishment.

"But I shall not embarrass you with a declaration in public," he assured her. "I can only hope that my suit will be furthered by my consideration."

Stacy smiled uneasily at him, and she was thankful

when the music started. The steps of the dance brought them together only infrequently, a fact that Stacy was extremely grateful for. She no more wanted a declaration from Mr. Granger than she did from Jeremy.

When the dance was over, Mr. Granger dutifully brought her back to Lady Elinor's side. Stacy had barely been seated when Jeremy mysteriously appeared again.

"May I have the next dance?" he begged pitifully.

Stacy glanced across the room and saw that Cecilia was watching them. Although the other girl looked away almost immediately, Stacy knew she was very conscious of everything that Jeremy did. Stacy made up her mind quickly.

"I'd like to go over to say hello to Cecilia and her grandmother," she told Jeremy.

He was far from pleased. "Can't we dance instead?" he pleaded.

But Stacy was firm. "I want to speak to her. If you've already greeted her, then you needn't come with me."

She could tell by Jeremy's blush that he had avoided Cecilia thus far, so she stood up, waiting for him. He got up and grudgingly led her across the floor.

"Hello, Cecilia," Stacy said happily, settling down in the chair next to her. "We wanted to come over and visit with you." Her nod indicated that it was

Jeremy's wish also, but his impatient attitude belied her words.

Cecilia greeted them quietly, but Stacy saw how Jeremy's attitude hurt her, and she wanted to kick him. "Isn't Almacks lovely?" she said instead. "I do love to dance, don't you?" she asked Cecilia.

"Yes," she said, then turned to watch the couples getting in place for the next set.

"Let's go, Stacy," Jeremy whispered impatiently.

Stacy gave him an angry look. "If you want to dance so badly, why don't you ask Cecilia?" she demanded.

Stacy turned back to her friend, only to find Cecilia watching her with a sad smile on her face, as if she had heard the interchange. Turning to Jeremy, she said, "Could you get us each a glass of orgeat, please? Dancing is such thirsty work," she added with a laugh.

Jeremy trudged across the floor toward the refreshment room, while Stacy watched him crossly.

"You didn't have to drag him over here, you know," Cecilia said quietly.

Stacy looked shamefaced that it had been so obvious. "I didn't really force him," she said defensively.

Cecilia smiled at her. "You have come to the wrong conclusion somewhere. Jeremy and I are close friends but nothing more," she insisted with a laugh. "I'm afraid I know him too well to want anything more of him."

Stacy's eyes narrowed suspiciously. "That's not how it seemed a few days ago."

The other girl shook her head. "Oh, a lot can change in a few days," she laughed quietly. "I must have been feeling shy then, and afraid to meet new people. I've discovered since then that there are other men in the world."

She sounded so confident that Stacy almost believed her, until she saw the way Cecilia's eyes lit up when she saw Jeremy coming back across the room.

Stacy tapped her foot impatiently, watching Jeremy with narrowed eyes. Someone was behind this little masquerade of Cecilia's, and she had a good idea who it was.

Jeremy had almost reached them when Cecilia stood up. "I do hope you will excuse me, but I did promise this dance, and it is one I don't want to miss." She smiled at Stacy, then turned to Jeremy. "You really ought to be dancing with Stacy instead of running about with glasses of that horrible orgeat. How anyone can drink it is beyond me . . ." She gave her most dazzling smile to a young man who had just come over to her, and allowed him to lead her away.

"What am I supposed to do with this?" Jeremy asked Stacy in exasperation, waving the glasses of almond-flavored drink in his hands.

"Wasn't that Mr. Sheridan that Cecilia went off with?" Stacy asked him, following the couple with her eyes.

Jeremy shrugged and put the glasses on a small table near their chairs. "Does it matter?" he asked, pulling out a white linen handkerchief. He carefully wiped the sticky drink from his fingers before he turned back to Stacy.

"But she hates him," Stacy cried. "Why would she dance with him and pretend to enjoy it so?"

Jeremy turned and looked for the couple. It was true that Cecilia seemed to be enjoying herself. She was laughing happily, and flashing her eyes toward him when they were separated. "She appears to have changed her mind about him," he said, not sounding totally pleased with the idea. He watched their by-play for a few minutes, then led Stacy away in disgust.

Depositing Stacy next to Lady Elinor with a singular lack of grace, he disappeared into the crowd. Just before he was lost to her sight, Stacy noted with wry humor that he was still watching Cecilia and Mr. Sheridan.

"Don't tell me you've been abandoned by all your admirers," Lady Elinor said, seeing Stacy by herself for the first time.

Stacy grinned. "I must have lost all my charm."

Lady Elinor snorted. "The men must have lost all their senses. When Anthony comes, I'll see that he shows them what they've been missing."

Stacy looked startled. "Oh, please don't tell him to

dance with me," she pleaded. "I'm sure he's had quite enough of me as it is."

The old lady said nothing, but she was surprised by Stacy's violent outburst. She had thought they had gone beyond the stage of wanting to avoid each other. She watched in silence as Stacy gazed at the dancers. She heard Stacy's sigh and sensed her restlessness.

"You don't seem to be having much fun tonight," she finally noted. "Would you rather go home?"

Stacy jumped at the chance. "Oh, yes, if you don't mind," she said. "I don't know why, but it does seem awfully flat tonight."

"I noticed that too," Lady Elinor noted, hiding a grin. "Something must be missing. Or someone," she added quietly.

Stacy stood up, shook the skirt of her dress slightly, and let the soft material float gently around her ankles. Lady Elinor gathered her things together and bid good-bye to the friends she had been sitting with. Stacy let her eyes wander over the couples dancing, enjoying the sound of the music.

Suddenly her eyes stopped on a figure near the door. She watched as he greeted Mrs. Drummond-Burrell, then turned and spoke to Lady Jersey, who smiled at him and laid her hand on his arm fondly.

Then Anthony turned around and looked across the room straight into Stacy's eyes. It was as if the rest of the room had disappeared and they were alone together. Music began to play from somewhere near them, but his eyes never left hers.

Slowly he walked across the room toward her, and she stood waiting. In a blinding flash she realized that she loved him. He was everything in the world that mattered to her, and when he stopped a few feet away from her, she went into his arms without a word.

Anthony had spent the best part of the evening staring into the fire in his parlor and drinking port. The more he had tried to erase the sight of Stacy and Laurie together, the more it seemed to haunt him. Finally, he had dressed for Almacks, hoping that activity would drive her from his mind.

Once he had greeted the patronesses, Anthony turned around, intending to look for Blanche and her mother, but the only one he saw was Stacy. He heard a waltz beginning and knew that it was being played for them.

As he had walked toward her he had almost imagined that he could see love in her eyes and her smile, for there was such an air of expectation about her. He must have asked her to dance, but he never remembered speaking. All he had known was a terrible need to hold her in his arms.

They moved around the room with the music, Anthony longing to pour out his heart to her but content to gaze into her eyes. For the moment there was no one else, and he could dream that she was his and he would never have to give her up.

When the music stopped, he dropped his arms slowly, reluctantly. Other couples brushed past them and intruded into their dreamworld. He stepped back from her and looked around them. Blanche came into focus abruptly. Her angry scowl was a cruel welcome to reality.

He turned back to Stacy, her eyes downward and her face carefully free of expression. Without a word he took her arm and led her across the floor, searching frantically for his grandmother. He spotted her with relief.

"I must join Blanche," he said, his voice harsh with embarrassment.

He nodded to Lady Elinor, thanked Stacy quickly, and almost ran away. Stacy watched him bitterly. It had been a perfect dance, a dream that had lasted as long as the music; then he had broken the spell by reminding her of Blanche.

"He was in a hurry," Lady Elinor noted, watching Stacy.

Stacy merely turned to pick up her shawl from the chair she had sat in. "Do you think we could go now?" she asked, barely controlling her anger.

CHAPTER ELEVEN

Laurie turned the corner, and the Johnson house came into view. His steps became quicker in happy anticipation of seeing his beloved Althea. He begrudged the hours that he had to be away from her, and he spent that time reliving the moments he had had with her.

If Laurie had had his way, they would have spent some part of each day together, but Althea said it was too much of an imposition. No matter how hard Laurie tried to assure her that nothing was as important as spending time with her, she insisted that he only come every few days.

The first time, Laurie had taken her shopping. Then they had gone for a walk in the park. One day they had stayed at her home and had tea while her dragon of a housekeeper looked on. Today was a beautiful, sunny day, and Laurie had definite plans. He had money in his pocket, and with it he was going to rent a carriage and take her for a drive through the park. Maybe they would even go to Hampton Court and try to find their way through the maze.

Laurie raised his hand to knock on the door but stopped before he touched the wood. The door was open a tiny crack. He pushed at it gently with the tips of his fingers. It swung open silently; the hallway beyond was shadowed and still.

He took a step into the house, a sense of foreboding sending a chill through his body. The sound of his boots on the wooden floor echoed loudly through the house, only increasing the feeling of desolation that he sensed.

"Althea!" he called tentatively as he moved farther into the house.

The stillness seemed almost a tangible thing, and he tried to move softly, for every noise screamed through the empty rooms and sent shivers down his spine. He pushed open the door of the sitting room they had used. The hinges creaked loudly in protest, but the room itself was deserted, the shabbiness of its furniture magnified without Althea's fragile beauty to distract one.

Laurie backed slowly out of the room and, in the hallway, knocked against a rickety table. A tarnished brass urn rocked precariously near the edge of the table, and Laurie made a grab for it. In doing so, he knocked the table even more, and the urn crashed to the floor, clattering along the boards until it came to rest against the bottom stair.

Laurie grabbed it guiltily and tried to balance it once more on its table. A large dent now adorned one side, and it leaned in lopsided splendor toward the edge of the table. Rather than risk another mishap, Laurie turned it upside down and walked back toward the door.

As he neared it, a small scuffling noise came from somewhere above him. He stopped moving and turned his head slightly, listening for the sound again. It was repeated a few moments later.

Cautiously Laurie walked back toward the stairs. Visions of robbers and murderers scuffling upstairs seemed more real to him than mice scurrying along the floor. Only the thought of his Althea being in danger forced him slowly up the stairs.

He did not hear the noise again and felt a little braver as he stood on the landing at the top. He looked about him, trying to decide if he should investigate further. He took a few steps forward and heard another noise. This one was more like a soft cry, and he was certain it was Althea's voice.

Forgetting his fear, Laurie rushed toward the sound and pushed open the door that stood in his way.

"Althea!" he cried as he looked with horror into the room. His lovely Althea lay on the floor next to an overturned chair. Her face was as pale as her lace-trimmed white dress, and her hair lay about her head in disarray, like gold spilled across the dark floor.

As he rushed over to her side, her eyelids fluttered open and she moaned slightly.

"Althea!" he cried, taking her hand and looking down into her eyes. Although her eyelids were not red, tears could be seen on her cheeks. "What happened?"

"Oh, Laurie!" she sighed softly. "Thank God you're here." Her head fell weakly to the side, and she closed her eyes for a moment.

Laurie looked about in panic. He gently put her hand down, and rose to his feet, intending to seek help, but she opened her eyes again.

"Laurie?" she called weakly, a thread of fear noticeable in her voice.

He fell to his knees again and clutched her hand. "I'm here," he reassured her.

Althea closed her eyes again, but tried to talk. "I fell," she whispered. "I was trying to reach something and I fell from the chair."

"Don't try to talk," Laurie warned her. "Don't even try to move. I'll get someone to help you."

Althea's eyes flew open. "No, no," she cried, grabbing at his coat in terror. "Please don't go," she pleaded. "I've lain here for hours and no one came. Please don't leave me alone anymore."

Laurie tried to soothe her. "Let me get your housekeeper," he said quietly. "I'll hardly be gone at all. I'll just call down the stairs for her."

Althea shook her head, wincing in pain at the movement. "She's gone for the day." The words came out in gasps.

"But you can't just lie here on the floor," Laurie cried. "You need a doctor."

She looked beyond him to her bed. "If you could just help me to my bed," she said, "I think I would be all right until you came back with someone."

Laurie tried to measure the distance with his eyes, knowing he was not very strong. He went over to the bed and pulled back the covers, then returned to Althea's side. He lifted her small body gently and carried her over to the bed. He laid her on the sheets, as carefully as he could, and began to pull the blanket over her.

"My shoes," she whispered with a weak smile. "If you could take them off . . ."

Laurie cursed himself for not thinking of what she needed to be comfortable. He pulled back the covers again and gingerly slipped her shoes off. Then he pulled the blanket up to her chin.

Althea smiled up at him. "You are so kind," she whispered.

Laurie sat down on the edge of the bed. "I won't

be gone long, I promise," he assured her. "And if I can't find someone quickly, I'll be back myself."

She nodded and whispered something that Laurie couldn't hear. He leaned over her, getting closer so that she would not have to strain her voice.

Once he was near her, Althea reached her arms up and put them around his neck. Laurie was startled and tried to draw back from her, but she held him tightly.

"Oh, Laurie, how I've waited for this moment," she sighed, trying to pull his head down closer to her.

"Althea!" Laurie cried in astonishment. "What are you doing? You've been hurt. You must lie still!" He reached up, trying unsuccessfully to loosen her hold.

One of her hands touched his hair softly, brushing it back from his face with a gentle caress. "You mustn't be so shy," she smiled, her voice a seductive whisper. The hand left his hair and tried to loosen the buttons on his shirt.

"Althea, please!" Laurie pleaded frantically. There seemed to be no way to avoid her hands. "I have to find a doctor."

"What do we want him here for?" she teased. She had succeeded in opening a part of his shirt, and she slid her hand inside, her fingers lying amid the hairs on his chest. "It's so much cozier with just the two of us." She sat up and covered his face with quick little kisses.

Laurie was panic-stricken by this time, certain that her fall must be responsible for her strange behavior. "You need help," he tried to reason with her, attempting to ignore the feelings her fingers were arousing in him. "Althea! Don't do that!" he cried suddenly.

She had managed to open his shirt completely, and she laughed quietly in triumph, pushing his cravat out of the way. Her fingers trailed sensuously over his skin. "Don't be so proper," she scolded lightly. "Don't you want to kiss me?"

"Well, of course," Laurie stammered nervously. "But I really think I should get the doctor for you."

She pouted prettily up at him. "Give me a kiss first," she demanded. "Then if you really want to go, I'll let you."

Laurie bent down uneasily to meet her lips. Further argument would only mean more time before a doctor came, so he gave in to her demand, intending to kiss her quickly, then leave. She had other ideas, though. As soon as he bent his head down she wrapped her arms tightly around his neck, making it impossible for him to move.

"My God! You shall pay for this!" The bedroom door was thrown open and crashed against the wall. Thomas Johnson stood in the doorway, a brute of a man ready to defend his sister's honor.

"It's not what you think," Laurie hastened to assure him as he moved away from the bed. "Althea fell, and I was helping her."

"Don't try that poppycock with me!" Thomas thundered, advancing across the room toward Laurie.

Laurie backed away timidly until he was up against a dresser. He put his hand back to steady himself and touched something soft. He glanced at it and saw that it was a stocking. His hand flinched away from it as if it burned.

"Tell him what happened," Laurie appealed to Althea. Thomas was pushing up the sleeves of his shirt.

"Why lie?" Althea laughed softly and slipped out of bed. As her feet touched the floor, she realized that she had no shoes on and laughed coquettishly. "Naughty boy!" she teased, and picked up her shoes. She sat on the edge of the bed and slipped her feet into them. "You are home much sooner than we expected," she said to Thomas with a laugh.

Laurie stared at her in horror. "What are you talking about?" he said, his voice cracking with fear.

She stood up again and walked over to her brother, slipping her arm around his. "You mustn't be so hard on him," she scolded Thomas lightly. "It was just a bit of fun."

Her laughter seemed to take some of the violence out of her brother, but his attitude toward Laurie was far from friendly. "You know what this means, don't you?" he snarled at him.

Laurie shook his head uncertainly, realizing suddenly that his shirt was open. He hurried to close it.

"You've ruined my little sister, and you'll have to pay for it."

Laurie stood staring at him, still trying to understand why Althea had lied. What was she trying to gain? "You mean I must marry her?" Laurie gasped.

Thomas shrugged a little and seemed to back down slightly. He shook his head wearily and went over to the bed. He sat down heavily on the edge.

"I like you, son," Thomas said slowly, "and I can see that you aren't ready for marriage, but what else can I do?" He spread his hands out in appeal. "Her reputation is ruined. Everyone in London will find out, and she'll never have a chance to make a decent marriage. We could leave London, I suppose, but we've just settled here, and it would take a lot of money to go somewhere else and start over . . ." Thomas's voice died away suggestively, and he covered his face with his hands.

Laurie watched him nervously, realizing that his future lay in this man's hands. Laurie coughed slightly. "Er, just how much do you think you would need?" he asked hesitantly, not wanting to offend.

Thomas looked up quickly. "Maybe ten thousand," he suggested.

Laurie turned white. "Ten thousand pounds?" he gasped. "I don't have that kind of money."

"I know you don't," Thomas said, rising and putting his arm around Laurie's shoulders. "But your brother does. You talk to him, and we'll come to see him tomorrow morning. I'll wager he thinks it's a small sum to pay."

He led Laurie over to the door and toward the top of the stairs. "Don't forget now," he said grimly as Laurie hurried down the stairs and out the door. "We'll see you the first thing tomorrow morning."

Cecilia fidgeted nervously while watching the man before her. "I really am sorry," she said, "but I have plans already. They just slipped my mind when you asked me to go driving."

Philip Sheridan frowned at her. "You did promise," he said in his whiny little voice.

Cecilia laughed slightly and glanced toward her grandmother, hoping the older woman would come to her rescue. Mrs. Frayne just smiled blandly at her.

With a sigh Cecilia edged toward the door. "It was kind of you to call. Maybe we could go out some other time."

But he was impervious to her suggestions and was still solidly planted in the middle of the drawing room, eyeing her with interest. "I would be happy to wait until you are free," he offered gallantly.

"That is quite kind of you." Mrs. Frayne smiled

innocently, ignoring the black look from her grand-daughter.

Cecilia shuddered. What had she done to encourage him last night? She wished fervently that she had not been quite so anxious to impress Jeremy.

"I had promised to call on Miss Prescott," she said, grasping the first excuse that came to mind.

"Well, that is no problem," he smiled eagerly. "I can easily take you there."

Cecilia shook her head, trying to be polite. "I would have to change first, and I could not ask you to wait."

Mr. Sheridan brushed aside the problem. "How long can that take?" He looked around him and spotted a comfortable chair near a window. "I shall be happy to wait," he announced as he settled himself in it.

All too soon they were riding along in Mr. Sheridan's curricle. He was under the impression that she found him irresistible, and he was acting accordingly. Although they were already crowded together, he kept moving closer, turning toward her each time he spoke so that his foul breath polluted the air, while his greedy little eyes leered at her. He patted her hand constantly, with a lingering caress. Cecilia practically jumped from the carriage when they stopped outside Lady Elinor's home.

Stacy was delighted to see Cecilia, although visibly startled to see her companion. To Cecilia's relief

Stacy did not reveal that the visit was unplanned, but invited them to be seated and sent a footman to tell Lady Elinor that they had guests.

"I didn't want to go driving with him," Cecilia whispered to Stacy as Lady Elinor engaged Mr. Sheridan in conversation. "I tried to refuse, but he's so buffleheaded, he did not understand."

Stacy was unsympathetic. "You weren't trying to be rid of him last night," she noted. "He must think you are besotted with him, the way you carried on."

Cecilia blushed and looked down at her hands. "That was different," she said miserably.

"Oh, yes," Stacy agreed sarcastically. "You were busy trying to impress someone then."

Cecilia glanced up at Stacy, her eyes filled with tears, and Stacy relented immediately. "Don't worry," she sighed, squeezing Cecilia's hand. "We'll find a way to discourage him."

After a discreet knock the butler appeared at the door. "Mr. Stephen Granger," he announced.

Conversation stopped, and everyone looked up as he entered. Mr. Granger seemed slightly taken aback to see that Stacy already had guests. He recovered himself quickly, however, and greeted Lady Elinor, then went to sit down near Stacy.

"I had hoped to find you alone," he told her, glancing meaningfully at Cecilia.

"Perhaps we ought to go," Cecilia suggested, moving uneasily.

Mr. Granger looked pleased, but Stacy shook her head. "You mustn't run off so soon," she scolded Cecilia. "You have only just arrived." Turning to Mr. Granger, she shook her finger playfully at him. "You shouldn't tease so," she told him. "Someone might take it seriously."

He smiled weakly with a shrug of his shoulders. Stacy laughed, treating it all as a joke, but Cecilia was worried. A quick smile from Stacy partly reassured her, while Mr. Granger settled back, prepared to wait.

Stacy determinedly kept the conversation going as they discussed parties—both upcoming and past—the latest fashion trends, sights to see in London, and horses. Lady Elinor watched with a twinkle in her eye as Stacy began a discussion of politics. It bothered Stacy not one bit that no one was even slightly interested, or that she knew nothing about the topic. Courtesy forced both men to respond when spoken to directly, and Cecilia quickly filled in any quiet moments with inane remarks.

"Maybe we ought to leave," Mr. Sheridan finally suggested, jumping into the middle of Stacy's opinion of trade with India.

"Not yet," Lady Elinor scolded. "Stacy wasn't finished." She bit back a laugh at Mr. Sheridan's chagrined expression, and looked up as another knock sounded at the door.

"Mr. Jeremy Chetwin," the butler announced.

Jeremy stopped just inside the room and frowned at the people there. Mr. Granger chuckled quietly, assuming that he, also, had hoped to find Stacy alone, but Stacy thought his frown had been directed more at Mr. Sheridan and Cecilia.

Cecilia must have thought so too, for she jumped nervously to her feet. "I think we ought to go," she said to Mr. Sheridan with a smile.

He rose eagerly and offered her his arm. "That was my thought exactly, my dear," he said, patting her hand lovingly.

Jeremy's frown deepened, but he said nothing, moving aside with a curt nod as they approached the door. Once they had left, he walked across the room and threw himself into the place Cecilia had just vacated.

"I hadn't realized that she was so keen on him," he grumbled, scowling at the closed door.

Stacy was disgusted with him. "You can't really believe that she is!" she snapped. How could he be so crackbrained as to not know who Cecilia really cared about?

"It is immaterial to me whom she cares for," he shrugged. He suddenly noticed Mr. Granger's presence with a frown. "I came to ask you to go for a drive," he told Stacy, eyeing the other man suspiciously.

"I'm afraid I was here first," Mr. Granger said with a smile.

"Then perhaps it's time you took yourself off," Jeremy said rudely.

Stacy turned angrily toward Jeremy, but Mr. Granger only smiled again and leaned back farther in his chair. "If you are going to be unpleasant, then you should be the one to leave," she scolded him.

Jeremy looked a trifle ashamed, and coughed nervously. "Have you been to see the Elgin Marbles?" he asked politely.

"Too late, Jeremy," Lady Elinor cackled. He looked blankly over at her. "We have covered that topic already."

He looked discomfited for a moment, then turned back to Stacy. "Blanche is looking forward to seeing you at her ball."

This time Mr. Granger snickered. "We have discussed that, too."

Jeremy tried hard to control his anger as the butler appeared at the door again. "Lord Anthony Kendall," he announced.

"What's this?" Anthony laughed when he saw the two men already there. "Are you taking on boarders, Grandmother?" He walked over and kissed her on the cheek, then sat down across the room from Stacy and her admirers.

"What brings you over here so early?" Lady Elinor asked suspiciously. "And so cheerful. I thought you only came when we had to be taken to task for our sins."

Anthony laughed. "Surely I'm not as grumpy as all that," he chuckled.

His grandmother watched him warily as he turned to the others. "Actually," he said. "I've come to take Stacy for a ride."

"Just get in line," Lady Elinor told him, chortling with delight.

Anthony looked at the other gentlemen in surprise, then at Stacy, but she said nothing. Although her heart had leapt at the thought of going out with him, she had not forgotten or forgiven him for leaving her so abruptly for Blanche last night. Did he think she was a puppet that could be picked up when wanted, or left forgotten if something better was available?

"I'm sorry," Stacy said sweetly, with a hint of anger in her voice. "But Mr. Granger has the first claim."

To her dismay, Mr. Granger stood up and shook his head. "I will quite gladly relinquish my spot to Lord Kendall, if he will grant me a few minutes of his time later today." Anthony stared at him blankly while Mr. Granger continued more quietly, "I was going to approach Miss Prescott herself about this matter, but I can see that you are acting as her guardian while she is here in town, so it would be better to discuss it with you first."

Mr. Granger's meaning finally penetrated, and Anthony froze at the thought of Stacy's marriage.

"Today is rather busy," he stammered. "Perhaps later in the week."

Mr. Granger nodded, not adverse to postponing the meeting, which only infuriated Anthony more and made him determined that Granger would never have Stacy, regardless of her feelings.

Anthony watched Mr. Granger leave the room, then turned to Jeremy, who was still sulking next to Stacy. "Are you still here?" he asked rudely.

Stacy jumped to her feet and glared at Anthony. "You have no right to be so rude to my guests," she cried.

Anthony's lips twisted sarcastically. "Don't tell me he's another stray lamb you have to protect," he snapped at her. Leaning closer to Jeremy, he warned, "She has a compulsion to defend anyone to whom I speak harshly. I would hate to see you mistake her pity for the downtrodden for any stronger feeling."

Stacy was ready to choke Anthony as Jeremy looked about him uncomfortably. "Perhaps I had better go," he mumbled, and hurriedly slipped out.

Lady Elinor saw the warring light in Stacy's eyes, and followed him to the door. "I'll just leave you two to your plans," she smiled, and closed the door behind her.

Anthony watched her leave and turned to Stacy. "Do you wish to change before we go?" he asked pleasantly.

"I'm not going anywhere with you," she cried, to

his total confusion. "What makes you think that you can waltz in here, rudely dismiss all my guests, and then expect me to be your companion for an hour?"

"I wasn't rude to Granger," he protested.

Stacy did not deign to notice his remark. "Why are you here, anyway?" she demanded. "Was Blanche too busy to go with you?"

"What does she have to do with any of this?" he shouted back at her.

Stacy sniffed haughtily and walked over to a window. "You make it very clear that you prefer Blanche's company, and you only honor us with your presence when she is already occupied."

"Perhaps that is because she knows how to carry on a polite conversation without turning it into a shouting match," he yelled, too furious to point out her error.

Stacy turned to face him. "If she's so wonderful to be with, then why are you here at all?"

Anthony said nothing for a moment, glaring at her angrily; then he abruptly turned on his heel and stalked toward the door.

"Where are you going?" she cried, her anger evaporating.

"To call on Blanche, where else?" he snapped, pulling open the door.

Laurie had been about to enter, and stumbled into the room. He seemed immensely relieved to see his brother. "Oh, Anthony, I've got to talk to you!" he cried.

"Does it have to be now?" Anthony asked sharply.

Laurie seemed taken aback by his curtness and shook his head slowly. "No, I guess it can wait," he mumbled.

Anthony nodded and rushed out.

Laurie looked after his brother for a moment, then turned back to Stacy. She was staring out the window again, her back to the room.

"Stacy?" he called uncertainly.

She turned around, tears rolling silently down her cheeks.

"What's wrong, Stacy?" he asked with concern.

She just shook her head, wiping the tears away with the back of her hand. "Did you want something?" she asked quietly.

"No, no," he said slowly. "It'll keep." She turned back to the window as he shuffled from the room.

CHAPTER TWELVE

Lady Elinor watched as the footman poured more hot chocolate into her cup; then, after a nod from her, he glided from the room. She stirred her drink absently, her eyes on Stacy, who was pretending to eat the eggs on her plate.

"Have you made your decision yet?" the old lady asked her.

Stacy looked up in surprise. "What decision?"

"I thought that was why you had come to London —to choose a husband," Lady Elinor remarked innocently, putting down her spoon. "Have you picked one out yet?"

"No," Stacy said quickly. "I actually haven't given the matter much thought at all." She pushed all the eggs into the exact center of her plate with grim determination.

Lady Elinor picked up her cup thoughtfully. "That's funny," she said. "I was sure you had made your choice already."

Stacy's eyes flew up, but Lady Elinor was innocently drinking her hot chocolate. She drained the cup and put it down, then wiped her lips carefully with her napkin. Looking over at Stacy's plate she said, "If you don't want your eggs, just leave them. I shan't send you to your room in disgrace."

Stacy blushed as she looked down at her plate. She had mashed her eggs into an unappetizing mess. She pushed the plate away with a sigh and, putting her elbows on the table, rested her chin in her hands.

Lady Elinor pushed her chair away from the table and stood up. "You know," she told Stacy confidentially, "I don't think she's as much of a rival as you fear."

"I don't know what you mean," Stacy mumbled uncertainly, lowering her arms and looking across the table at Lady Elinor.

"Oh, yes, you do," the old lady said with a twinkle in her eye. "You're worrying about Blanche, when Anthony's going to be much more of a problem."

"In what way?" Stacy asked, her curiosity overcoming an inclination to deny everything.

Lady Elinor walked around the room, stopping near Stacy's chair. She gently pushed a stray curl off the young girl's forehead. "He's been fighting you all along." Stacy's lips tightened in memory of their argument yesterday, but Lady Elinor only laughed. "Not in that way," she said. "He's been fighting your attractions. But he's been so busy doing that, and losing, that he hasn't noticed how you feel about him. It will be up to you to make him notice." She reached out and touched the tip of Stacy's nose playfully. "You may have to choose between your pride and your love, so be warned."

She smiled at Stacy and went to the door, greeting Laurie, who was on his way in.

Laurie watched as his grandmother left the room, then hurried over to the chair next to Stacy and sat down. He showed no interest in the appetizing dishes on the sideboard, turning instead to her.

"Stacy, can we talk?" he pleaded.

A footman came in and offered to fill Laurie's plate for him, but he was impatiently waved back out of the room.

"I'm in terrible trouble," Laurie cried. "Anthony will disown me."

"Nonsense," Stacy said bracingly, but she noted Laurie's pale face and worried eyes and waited for him to confide in her.

"It's Althea," he said haltingly. "You remember I spoke of her?"

Stacy nodded her head slowly.

"I've compromised her!" he blurted out. "Her

brother says I must marry her." He looked as if he were ready to cry.

"What happened?" Stacy asked, stunned by his news.

"It was all a horrible mistake," he cried. "She fell, and I was just trying to help her. Suddenly she began to act very strange." His face turned red as he remembered her actions. "Then her brother rushed in and accused me of compromising her. He insisted that I marry her."

"Have you spoken to Anthony about it?" she asked, almost sure of the answer.

"How can I?" he cried, twisting his hands in anguish. "I had hoped that maybe you could," he added hopefully.

Stacy sat back in astonishment while Laurie nervously drew circles on the tablecloth with a fork.

"I know that you hate him," he went on, not looking at her, "but you aren't afraid of him. I thought that if you would talk to him, I could keep out of his way until he cools down a bit." He looked over at her anxiously, realizing that she had not spoken much.

"How could I tell him something like that?" Stacy said slowly. "This is something you will have to handle yourself."

"Oh, please, Stacy," he cried, looking so like a little boy that her heart nearly broke for him.

Dumbly she nodded. "I may see him tonight," she added. "If so, I'll try to talk to him alone."

Laurie shook his head. "No, it can't be then. You must go to see him now." Stacy wondered at his insistence. "Mr. Johnson is going to see him this morning," Laurie added in a low voice. "You must go now and warn him he's coming."

Stacy just stared at Laurie for a long moment. "Oh, Laurie," she sighed, and stood up.

He rose also, looking miserable and forlorn. Stacy reached over and hugged him. "It's all right," she assured him. "I'll fight this battle for you too."

Stacy pulled a pair of walking shoes from her wardrobe as Mary, her maid, rushed in.

"Oo, miss, I've got ta talk ta ya," she cried.

Stacy sat on her bed, putting her shoes on. "Must it be now?" she asked impatiently. "I am just going out."

Mary nodded. "I know," she said.

Stacy stopped what she was doing to look at her maid. "You do?" she asked.

"James the footman overheard what Master Laurie told ya. That's what I gotta talk 'bout."

Stacy knew that there were few things that could be kept from the servants, and she hoped they were trustworthy enough not to spread the story about. "What about Laurie?" she asked.

Mary started to straighten Stacy's dressing table as

she spoke. "It's 'bout them Johnsons," she began awkwardly. "Mr. Tooms, the butler, 'e knows 'em, or thinks 'e does."

"For goodness' sake, get on with it!" Stacy cried, impatient with her hesitations and qualifications.

Mary nodded and stopped folding scarves. She turned toward Stacy, her hands clenched in front of her. "Ya see, Mr. Tooms, 'e got this friend who worked for a family in Bath, and they 'ad a son 'bout Master Laurie's age. 'E met up with this woman named Althea, and she tricked 'im into compromising 'er, and then 'er brother rushes in."

"How does this help us?" Stacy snapped impatiently, not wanting to waste time listening to gossip.

"The brother, 'e ain't 'er brother at all, 'e's 'er 'usband," Mary said quickly. "And they ain't about ta marry the lad. They want the family to buy 'em off."

Stacy stared at her for a moment, unwilling to believe that Laurie was being used that way. "Are you sure it's the same people?" she whispered. "We can't just accuse them with no proof."

"Can we jest sit by and maybe let it 'appen to Master Laurie 'cause we ain't sure?" Mary cried.

"You are right," Stacy nodded as she jumped off her bed and grabbed her reticule, quickly tying a bonnet on her head. "I may not be able to accuse them without proof, but perhaps they might supply that proof for me," she murmured as an idea took shape in her mind.

It seemed to take hours for the carriage to go the few blocks to Anthony's home. As soon as it slowed to a stop, Stacy jumped out. She pressed a few coins into the driver's hand and rushed up the stairs, followed quickly by her maid. They ran past an astonished footman, but stopped short in the hallway as they came face to face with Anthony's butler.

"I must see Lord Kendall," Stacy gasped.

"He is occupied at the moment, but if you would care to wait in the parlor, I'll let you know when he is free." The butler kept his large frame blocking the library door, while his hand indicated a small parlor down the hall.

Stacy glanced quickly at Mary. She had not thought that they might be stopped at this point. Before Stacy's astonished eyes, Mary suddenly covered her mouth with her hands.

"I'm gonna be sick," she yelled out.

The butler and the footman rushed as one over to her side, moving her to a chair. In the confusion Stacy saw Mary wink at her, then return to her faint moaning. Stacy looked back at the butler. He was occupied and the door was free. She slipped inside.

Anthony was at his desk when she entered, writing something. He looked up and frowned when he saw who it was. There were two other people in the room

—a blond young lady, who had to be Althea, and a burly man who must be her husband. The man frowned when she entered, but his face relaxed when he saw that it was just a girl.

"What are you doing here?" Anthony demanded, rising to his feet. He held a piece of paper in his hand.

"I had to come," Stacy cried, her eyes on the paper. Was it a bank draft for their money?

"For God's sake, Stacy, not now," he snapped at her, then walked around his desk toward the man.

Without thinking, Stacy grabbed the paper from Anthony's hand and tore it into little pieces.

"What are you doing?" Anthony cried, making a futile grab for the pieces.

The large man had jumped to his feet. "You can't throw a rub in my way, Kendall," he growled.

Ignoring the two men, Stacy threw herself on her knees before Althea. "Laurie has told me everything," she said loudly enough for everyone to hear. "He has confessed it all to me just minutes ago." She bent her head slightly and sniffed loudly.

"Stacy," Anthony called her impatiently. When she did not respond, he put his hand on her arm to pull her up, but she stayed close to Althea, looking up at him in horror.

"No, it must be said," she told him. He stared at her blankly.

Stacy turned back to Althea. "He told me the

194

terrible thing he did to you, and he is so ashamed that he let his feelings override his good sense."

"We ain't listening to all this," Mr. Johnson complained. "Give us that money, or we might just change our mind and insist on the wedding."

Stacy looked up and saw Anthony walking back toward his desk. She turned back to Althea quickly. "But that's why I'm here," she said. "Laurie wants to marry you. He feels he must, and I agree with him."

"Stacy!" Anthony shouted. Hurrying around his desk, he grabbed her arm and tried to drag her across the floor. "Will you please be quiet?" he whispered furiously. "For once, trust me to know what is right!"

Stacy twisted away from him and took refuge behind a chair. "I have freed Laurie from his engagement to me, so that he is free to marry Althea." She dug in her reticule and pulled out a lace handkerchief. She dabbed at her eyes. "We love each other so much, but we could not be happy at her expense." She took advantage of the silence in the room to sob pitifully into her hankie.

"What about that money?" Johnson nudged Anthony impatiently.

Stacy sobbed even louder. "How can any amount of money make up for this girl's shame? What kind of a brother are you?" she scolded Thomas. "How can you put a price on her good name?"

"Stacy, please," Anthony pleaded.

She hurried across the room to Althea's side. "You must make him understand," she told the girl earnestly, clutching Althea's hands tightly. "Tell him how you feel about Laurie."

"But I . . . I . . ." Althea tried to free her hands.

"You needn't be shy." Stacy smiled bravely. "We understand how you feel. It was more than you dared hope for, and now, suddenly, to realize that you'll be marrying Laurie in just a few minutes . . ."

"What are you talking about?" Anthony shouted as Althea stood up, frantically trying to edge away from Stacy.

Stacy looked at Anthony. "Laurie's gone to get a special license," she said. "Then he's bringing a parson back here to perform the ceremony."

"He's what?" Althea cried faintly, falling back into her chair.

Anthony looked as startled as the Johnsons. "And whose idea was that?" he snapped.

"He can't do that," Thomas insisted loudly. "We want that money now, Kendall."

A noise from the outer hallway was heard in the room.

"Why, that must be Laurie and the minister now," Stacy cried, closing her eyes with a sob. "I don't know if I can bear to watch Laurie marry another."

"But I can't marry him," Althea cried, looking about her desperately.

Her brother made a sudden start. "Close your trap, you little fool!" he shouted.

Flying to her feet, Stacy stepped back from Althea in horror. "You can't marry him?" Stacy cried out. "Why can't you?"

Althea realized that she had made the fatal slip, and she looked to her brother worriedly. "She means she doesn't want to," he tried to explain, but Anthony stepped forward with a frown.

"If you both are so concerned about her reputation, then why doesn't she?" he demanded.

"Maybe we had better go," Althea suggested nervously as she turned to Stacy. "I don't want to ruin your plans," she said weakly. Stacy allowed her to slip by, and she and Thomas hurried out the door, closely followed by Anthony.

Stacy leaned back against a chair. She felt exhausted but quite happy. Laurie was safe, and Anthony had not paid out the money they had wanted. She frowned as she realized one problem. All that sobbing had made her terribly thirsty.

Seeing that Anthony had a small liquor cabinet in the corner, she wandered over to it. She found nothing in it that she liked; there wasn't even a pitcher of water. She was closing the door when she spotted a bottle of brandy. She had always been curious about its taste, and gingerly pulled the bottle out.

It was very quiet in the hallway, so she assumed that no one was about. She took a glass out of the cabinet and quickly poured a little brandy into the bottom of it. Then she closed the bottle and replaced it.

She took a small sip and grimaced. It was terribly strong. She tried another sip and began to cough.

A hand reached around her and took the glass out of her hand. She turned, trying to stop coughing, and saw Anthony frowning at her. He sniffed at the glass.

"My God, this is brandy!" he said.

She nodded miserably, ashamed to have been caught with it.

Anthony gently took her hand and led her over to the sofa, still carrying the glass of brandy. "How thoughtless of me," he said, shaking his head. "This must have been a terrible ordeal for you."

She stared at him blankly while he sat her down and held the glass to her lips. "Drink it all," he coaxed. "It will make you feel better."

She tried to argue that she felt fine, outside of a small thirst, but the moment her mouth opened he tipped the brandy in. She coughed and spluttered most indelicately.

"That brother of mine is certainly a fool!" he said, barely concealing his rage. "He shouldn't even look at another woman when he has you." He frowned suddenly. "But then I suppose that was my fault, wasn't it?"

Stacy stared at him dumbly as he tried to reassure

her. "This was a terrible thing that happened, but it helped me reach a decision."

There were tears in the corner of her eyes from the brandy, but Anthony was sure they were caused by him. With a sad smile he gently wiped them away.

"I've decided to give you and Laurie my permission to marry," he told her quietly.

"What!" Stacy gasped, pulling away from him.

Anthony stood up, turning briefly away. "I realized when I saw how upset you were, how much you must love him. It took such courage to come here, prepared to give him up for another just because you knew that his conscience would not allow him to be happy."

"What are you talking about?" Stacy demanded.

Anthony turned back to her. "About your love for Laurie," he said.

Stacy sighed loudly and got to her feet. "Haven't you realized that it was all a trick?" she asked. "Althea and Thomas only wanted money. Laurie didn't really compromise her."

Anthony stared at her questioningly. "I realized it at the end, yes," he said, then stopped. "You mean you knew it when you came in?"

Stacy nodded, and Anthony said nothing for a long moment. Then he went over to his desk. "Then all that about loving Laurie was a trick too?" he asked, leaning heavily on his hands.

Stacy looked at him anxiously. She could not see

his face, and his voice was carefully under control. Was he ready to blaze out at her?

"Not all of it, no," she said slowly. "You see, I do love Laurie." He looked up at her, and his eyes seemed to be full of pain. "But not in the way I led them to believe," she went on.

Anthony straightened up and moved closer to her. "In what way, then?" he asked.

Stacy twisted her hands together in front of her uncertainly, keeping her eyes down. "When we eloped, I told him that I loved him, and I thought I did," she hurried to add. "But I know now that it was a different kind of love. It was the love for a brother, or a close friend, not the love that you have for someone you want to marry."

"How can you be so sure?"

Stacy looked up, startled. She had not known he was so close to her. She gazed nervously into his eyes.

"Have you felt both kinds of love?" he asked.

His eyes beseeched her for an answer, but she was afraid to admit her love. Then she remembered Lady Elinor's words. It was her pride holding her back, but her love was more important.

"Yes," she nodded, her eyes locked with his. "I have felt both kinds of love. I love Laurie very much, but I love his brother far more."

Anthony gave a soft cry and pulled her into his arms. "Oh, Stacy," he whispered into her hair. "I never thought this was possible. I've loved you for so long, but I never thought there was any hope for me."

Stacy laughed softly, and pulled back slightly so that she could look up into his eyes. "Do you mean you actually love me too?" she asked in wonder.

The laughter in their eyes died suddenly as passion took its place. Anthony's lips came down to meet hers. Stacy's arms went around his neck, holding him as she kissed him back freely, their need for each other before all else.

Stacy's heart was pounding as he rained kisses on her lips and her eyelids. She sighed as the tip of his tongue tickled her ear, and shivered with delight as he kissed the little hollow at the base of her neck. She burrowed deeper and deeper into his embrace.

Suddenly the glimpse of heaven was snatched away from her, and she stood alone. She opened her eyes slowly, stunned by the sudden emptiness. Anthony was standing a few feet away from her. He was leaning against a chair, his head down and his back to her.

Stacy took a step toward him. "Anthony?" she asked hesitantly.

He straightened up when she spoke, but did not face her. "It's no good," he said harshly.

She just stared at him, and slowly he turned around to face her, his hands still clasping the back of the chair.

"You will have to forget me," he said.

"But I thought you loved me," she whispered.

A look of pain crossed his face. "I do," he admitted, closing his eyes briefly. "But that doesn't matter."

Stacy felt as if she were being torn apart. "It does to me," she said, her agony quite visible.

Anthony turned his head, so that he was looking away from her. "You should never have come here today," he said curtly. "It would have been better to have paid the Johnsons their money and never have said what we did today."

Stacy clutched her hands together to stop their trembling. "You said you loved me," she repeated numbly.

"Don't you understand?" Anthony was driven to shout. "I'm marrying Blanche, so whatever I said means nothing. Nothing at all."

Stacy stared at him, the blood draining from her face. "You are going to marry her, even though we love each other?"

Anthony nodded slowly. "There's nothing I can do now. I asked her to marry me and she accepted. It doesn't matter if I've changed my mind. I have to marry her."

Stacy took a step closer to him. "But there hasn't been an announcement. Who would know if you broke the engagement?"

"You just do not understand," he sighed, and

walked briskly across the room to stare out the window. "A man of honor never breaks an engagement, even a private one. To do so would expose Blanche to a great deal of embarrassment."

"But how, if no one knows?" Stacy persisted.

"Everyone does know," Anthony snapped as he turned to face her. "It has been no secret that I have been courting Blanche, or that she looked upon my suit with favor. If I suddenly ignored her and turned my attention to you, she would be humiliated quite publicly."

Stacy's lips tightened angrily. "I see," she said. "So rather than let Blanche's feelings be hurt . . ."

"It isn't just Blanche," he pointed out quickly. "I would no longer be accepted in society. Oh, there'd be some loose fish who would not mind what I had done, but no respectable hostess would issue an invitation to me, and I would no longer be welcome at my clubs. Then when I showed partiality toward you, you would also be shunned. They'd label you as one who plays fast and loose, and the doors of Almacks would be closed to you forever."

Stacy watched him impatiently. "Do you really think Almacks is that important to me?"

"Maybe not now," he shrugged, "but after a few years in the country, knowing that you cannot take your place in society, you would change your mind."

"That's ridiculous!" she snapped. "I never had any

desire to come to London. I was perfectly happy in the country, and could be again."

Anthony did not look convinced. He walked back to his desk and began to sort idly through some papers. "That may be so," he admitted, his voice sounding cold and unfeeling, "but since I am marrying Blanche, the question does not arise."

Stacy took another step forward, then stopped. He had made it very clear that he wanted to marry Blanche, not her, and her pride forbade her to demean herself any further by begging him to reconsider. "I see," she said slowly. He did not look up from his papers. "Then there is nothing else to say."

He did not argue the point, saying nothing as she quietly left the room.

CHAPTER THIRTEEN

After much painful deliberation, Anthony presented himself at the Chetwin house later that morning. He was not convinced that he was doing the right thing, but the thought of losing Stacy was too much for him to bear, and he realized that he had to make an attempt, at least, to be free of his engagement.

When Blanche joined him in the parlor, he could see that his timing had not been good. She had been involved in settling some domestic affairs and was not pleased to have been called away from them.

"I did not expect to see you this morning," she noted coldly as she sat down.

Anthony sat down across from her and smiled

weakly. "I hope that my visit has not inconvenienced you," he said.

She shrugged, but did not deny it.

There was a moment of awkward silence while Anthony thought frantically how he might begin. Blanche watched him suspiciously.

"I have been giving our marriage a great deal of thought," he began. "About where we shall live, and how we will get along . . ."

"Yes?" Her voice did not invite him to confess all to her.

He cleared his throat nervously. "You know, of course, that my parents were not happy together, and I would not want to repeat their mistakes. For either of our sakes," he added quickly.

"I can't see how we would," Blanche said in a slightly scolding tone. "We are ideally suited, and not afflicted with romanticism to disrupt our lives."

"Romantic attachment is not necessarily bad," Anthony said hesitantly. "Sometimes it develops without our knowledge."

Blanche frowned at him, then glanced around the room without speaking. She was not unaware of his fascination with Miss Prescott, and she had a very clear idea of what this whole conversation was about. She was not kindly disposed toward lovers, however, and certainly not about to change her plans just because he found himself enamoured of someone else.

"In spite of your concern that we may not be

suited, I am well aware of the real reason behind this discussion," she said. "I would have had to be totally blind not to notice the amount of attention that you pay to Miss Prescott. No doubt you have convinced yourself that if you could just marry her, you would be happy."

Although she had spoken in a forbidding tone, Anthony looked up hopefully. Surely, knowing the truth about his feelings, she would release him from their engagement. "I did not want it to happen," he told her apologetically.

Blanche stood up and walked across the room. There she stopped and turned around to watch him. "I can understand how it may have occurred," she said more calmly. "She is attractive, in a youthful way, and her artlessness can be refreshing at first. However, I pride myself on being quite realistic, and I know that once we are married there will be times when you find yourself attracted to some other female. It does not bother me now, and it shall not bother me then."

"Once we are married . . . ?" he repeated dumbly.

"Surely, you did not expect me to change all our plans just because of this temporary attraction you feel," Blanche laughed. "I can remember your true feelings toward the girl, even if you cannot. You may think she is lovely now, but in a few months your real feelings will return, and you would be quite miserable if you were tied to her."

Anthony started to protest, but she waved him aside impatiently. "We are well suited, and that fact will not change," she told him. "After you experience several attacks of romanticism and see how quickly they disappear, you will be quite glad that you married me. We have no fleeting emotions to tie us together, or embarrass us when they have gone. We are alike in temperament and interests, and that will last far longer than this love you feel now."

Anthony's lips were tightened in irritation. "I see," he said quietly. "So you will not release me?"

"I am doing it for your own good," she reminded him. "I know what you want from life."

Anthony nodded curtly, realizing it was useless to argue with her any further. He should never have approached her about breaking the engagement—for he had known he was not being particularly honorable—but he had been so desperate. "I hope that I have not offended you," he said, turning to Blanche.

She shook her head with a slight smile. "Not at all," she assured him. "But if we are through, I do have other things to attend to."

After thanking her for her time, Anthony left.

Cecilia put down her needlework and looked up in surprise as Jeremy was shown into the room. Mrs. Frayne closed her book, leaving her finger marking her page, and glanced at the clock with a frown.

"This is an odd time to be calling," she scolded him. "We have to dress for dinner in a few minutes."

Jeremy seemed taken aback at his cool reception. "I wished to speak with Cecilia," he said hesitantly.

"Well, there she is," Mrs. Frayne said with a wave of her hand. Then she went back to her book.

Jeremy turned to Cecilia and found that she was watching him quizzically. Moving with sudden purpose, he walked across to where she sat and took the chair next to her.

"How is Stacy?" Cecilia asked as he leaned forward to speak.

Jeremy sat back with a frown. "She is fine, I imagine," he said with a shrug. "But that is not why I am here."

"Oh?" Cecilia asked. She looked down at her sewing, methodically picking out the last few stitches. "Then why are you here?"

Jeremy's lips narrowed impatiently at her inattention, and his eyes darted over to Mrs. Frayne, who appeared to be reading avidly. This was hardly the setting he wanted for this conversation. He leaned forward, resting his arms on his knees.

"I don't like this Sheridan fellow," he blurted out. "He's a queer fish if I ever saw one."

Cecilia's hands stopped for a moment in surprise, but her eyes remained on her work. "I am afraid I don't see why you are telling me this," she said quietly.

"Don't play coy," he cried angrily. "Every time I look around, you are with the fellow. You seem quite taken with him of late."

"Your opinion of Mr. Sheridan does not interest me in the least," she said coldly. "It may come as a shock to you, but I am old enough to have a home and family of my own. Is it so strange that I should accept the company of someone who might give them to me?"

Jeremy was stunned. "But that's ridiculous," he cried loudly. Remembering Mrs. Frayne, he glanced guiltily over at her. She was staring at him over the top of her book. He smiled a weak apology and turned back to Cecilia. "You talk as if you are on the shelf. Why, you're younger than I am."

Cecilia looked up, and shrugged. "It's different for you," she pointed out. "A man may take as long as he pleases to choose a wife, but a girl has only one or two seasons to accept an offer, or she remains a spinster."

Jeremy's eyes opened wide. "You mean you are seriously considering marrying him?" he stammered.

"He hasn't asked me yet," Cecilia noted. "But if he did, yes, I would have to consider it."

"You must be insane," he said, falling back in his chair, shaking his head.

"Thank you," Cecilia said curtly. "And might I ask what business it is of yours?"

Jeremy looked hurt at her sharpness. "I thought we were friends, and I was concerned about you."

Cecilia looked skeptical. "Do you mean you were concerned or Blanche was? I'll wager that Blanche was behind this little visit."

"No, she wasn't," Jeremy cried quickly. A little too quickly, Cecilia thought angrily.

"Oh, do stop, Jeremy," she said, tossing her sewing onto the table in front of her and standing up. "You made it very clear to me the other day that I was in your way and that Blanche's manipulations were an embarrassment to you. As a result I have tried to stay away from you and not presume on the friendship that we shared as children. Now you will just have to do the same. If you do not want me in your life, then you must stay out of mine."

She angrily picked up the threads that she had scattered about her and stuffed them into her sewing basket. "It is absolutely no concern of yours who I am seen with or not seen with. You may smile at whomever you want, and I will do the same."

Jeremy jumped up, catching her shoulders to make her stand still as he spoke to her. "So that's what's behind all this. You're upset about what I said the other day," he marveled.

She twisted out of his arms and slipped around the table, glaring at him across it. "You flatter yourself if you think that any words of yours could cause me distress for more than a few minutes," she snapped.

"Now, if you are quite finished, we have plans for this evening and would like to dress."

Jeremy watched her in silence as she sought to regain her control. Her cheeks were flushed and her chest was heaving from her rapid breathing.

"Are you attending Lord Attenborough's card party?" he asked. "Perhaps I will see you there."

She shook her head with a harsh laugh. "You needn't worry that I shall expect you to speak to me, because I won't be there," she said with a hint of triumph. "Philip is taking us to see *As You Like It* at the Drury Lane Theatre."

A frown crossed Jeremy's face. "But you have already seen that play with me," he said.

Cecilia shrugged and then smiled at Jeremy's look of rage. "I'm afraid that I don't remember a great deal about the show," she said sweetly. "My escort was so busy ogling another young lady that it rather spoiled the evening for me."

Jeremy's face paled, and he stepped back as if stung. "I did not," he protested.

"Tonight, at least," she continued, "I can be sure that I shall have Philip's attention."

"Attention?" He tried to strike back at her. "Is that what you call his leers?"

Cecilia refused to be drawn into another argument. "If I do not find him offensive, why should you?"

"There's just no reasoning with you," Jeremy exclaimed in disgust.

Cecilia stared straight ahead of her, avoiding his eyes. "I think you had better go," she said quietly, "before whatever friendship we have is lost forever."

He walked around the small table and past her. He stopped for a second, his hand raised as if to try to reason with her, but she did not even glance at him. His hand fell, and he continued walking to the door.

Just as he was about to leave, Cecilia spoke again. "And Jeremy," she said coldly, "you can tell Blanche that I will make chair covers when I want to and can choose the pattern without her help!"

Jeremy pulled the door open. "Good-day," Mrs. Frayne called out gaily.

He had forgotten that she was there, and he looked over at her, his face scarlet, and nodded. Then he turned sharply on his heel and left.

There was complete silence in the room for several minutes after they heard the outside door close. Cecilia remained standing rigidly where she had been.

"I hadn't realized that your feelings for Mr. Sheridan ran so deep," Mrs. Frayne noted, putting her book down next to her.

"I detest him," Cecilia said with a sigh. She picked up her needlework, carefully folding it, and placed it on the top of her sewing basket. She sat down on the edge of the sofa and looked across at her grandmother with stricken eyes, but the older woman was smiling. "He is the most repulsive man I've ever met," Cecilia added with feeling.

"Mr. Sheridan or Jeremy?"

Cecilia had to smile in spite of herself. "I really flew into him, didn't I?" she smiled. "But he has made his choice. He wants Stacy, so he has to let me find someone else."

"But you don't want Mr. Sheridan," her grandmother pointed out.

"No, but I never said I did. All I did was dance with him, and Jeremy is screaming at me. He came in here with false assumptions and insulted my intelligence. He deserved to hear some home truths."

Mrs. Frayne shook her head with a laugh. "I think he wondered what happened to the mouse he used to know."

Cecilia stood up and looked at her grandmother with a smile. "The mouse has decided to grow wings and fly," she declared.

"Good!" Mrs. Frayne nodded. "Now maybe you can tell me how we are going to survive an evening in the company of that detestable young man."

"I don't know why we have come," Laurie complained. "I would much rather have stayed at home."

Lady Elinor smiled at the butler, who took her shawl, then she moved toward the other guests.

"That is precisely why we came," she muttered under her breath to Laurie. "Left to your own devices, you two would have moped around all evening, and since no one wants to tell me what's wrong . . ." She paused a moment, looking meaningfully first at Stacy, then at Laurie, but neither of them rushed forward with confidences. Shaking her head with a frown, Lady Elinor continued, "So we are here, and we will enjoy ourselves."

The two nodded grimly and followed her along the hallway to greet their host, Lord Attenborough.

He was a small man, who nodded constantly as he spoke. "How nice to see you," he smiled, his head bobbing up and down with each word. He looked just beyond them with a wider smile. "Ah, there you are, Kendall. I wondered if you were escorting your ladies tonight."

Stacy turned her head slightly and saw Anthony standing behind them. She looked away quickly, her heart still aching from the way he had rejected her love earlier that day.

"Oh, God," Laurie moaned quietly to Stacy. "I hoped to stay away from him until he had a chance to calm down. I do not want to die yet."

Lady Elinor greeted Anthony with enthusiasm as they moved into Lord Attenborough's drawing room. "I'm so glad to see a cheerful face," she said, putting her arm through his and ignoring the fact that he looked far from happy. "Those two young people are glum enough to make a professional mourner look like a clown. Maybe you can cheer them up," she suggested.

Anthony looked over at Laurie, who was walking with Stacy on the other side of Lady Elinor. "I would be most happy to try," he assured her, putting a firm hand on his brother's arm.

Laurie, forced to stop, looked about him nervously. "I've been looking for you today," Anthony said warmly. He put pressure on his arm and moved Laurie away from the others. "I had expected that you would come to see me."

"I, . . . uh, . . . was out," Laurie said. He was watching the people in the room, but his eyes kept darting anxiously to Anthony's face.

"Visiting friends?" Anthony asked with a relentless smile.

Laurie ran a finger around the inside of the collar that suddenly threatened to choke him. "No, no," he cried. "I was seeing London. The Tower, Fleet Prison . . ." His voice weakened.

"Ah." Anthony nodded with sudden understanding. "You were looking at your future accommodations? Don't tell me that you skipped the Tyburn Tree?"

Laurie shook his head, muttering to himself. "I wanted to see some places before I went back to the country," he told his brother.

Anthony looked at him, his forehead creased in

bewilderment. "I didn't know you were leaving," he said. "I hope you weren't going without saying good-bye."

Laurie glanced up, a ray of hope lurking in his eyes. "Aren't you going to send me back?" he asked uncertainly.

Anthony said nothing for a moment, and the ray of hope began to flicker. Then he shook his head. "As certain people keep reminding me, you are growing older. Hopefully, you have learned from this experience and from now on will be a little more careful in choosing your companions."

"Oh, yes, I will," Laurie enthused, shaking Anthony's hand vigorously. "I won't talk to anyone, you'll see. I won't ever do anything idiotic again."

Anthony laughed. "I would be careful about promising that. I don't think any of us are totally immune from stupidity."

"Well, you don't seem to act as stupidly as I do," Laurie pointed out.

Anthony thought of his recent dealings with Stacy and of his self-imposed prison term with Blanche. "I may be the stupidest one of us all," he said. Seeing Laurie's surprise, he went on quickly, "I was surprised that you showed no interest in what happened today when your friends called on me."

Laurie blushed and looked down at his shoes. "Stacy told me what happened, so I wasn't worried."

"She told you everything that happened?" Anthony gasped.

Laurie looked up at his brother. "Not everything, I guess, from your expression." A frown settled on Laurie's face. "Don't tell me that you argued with her again!" he cried impatiently. "You must have known she had nothing to do with the Johnsons. I only asked her to see you because I was afraid to tell you myself." He looked away in disgust. "You seemed to be fairly pleasant to her lately, and I thought that your ridiculous dislike of her had passed. I only hope that she won't hold me responsible for your actions." He glared at his brother, and turned on his heel, striding away before Anthony could speak in his own defense.

As Anthony took Laurie off to one side, Lady Elinor smiled at them and joined Stacy. "However angry Anthony makes me, you cannot deny that he really cares about his brother."

Stacy nodded silently as she looked for her own method of escaping Anthony. Just the sight of him was enough to bring back vivid memories of his kisses and of her own declaration of love.

She had spent a great deal of time thinking about what had happened between her and Anthony that morning. In fact, she had done nothing but go over and over it in her mind. She had painfully dissected the entire conversation and had finally stumbled onto the truth.

Her own admission of love had upset him, and rather than embarrass her by telling the truth, he pretended to return her feelings. It was fortunate that he had Blanche to protect him, for by holding fast to his honor, he could sadly deny anything that she, Stacy, might want from him. The whole idea of Anthony pitying her so made her burn with mortification, and she vowed to disprove everything she had said to him that morning.

When she saw Jeremy walking along one side of the drawing room, she slipped away from Lady Elinor. She put her arm through Jeremy's and smiled up at him.

"Oh, hello, Stacy," he said unenthusiastically.

"You are quite lucky that I'm in a forgiving mood," she teased, "and won't take offense at that greeting." Glancing back where she had been, she saw Laurie leave Anthony's side. She quickly turned back to Jeremy. "Now tell me," she said with a smile, "why do you look so glum?"

He needed no second urging. "She's going to the theatre tonight with that Sheridan fellow," he complained. "And she was angry at me for pointing out his shortcomings!"

"I assume you mean Cecilia," Stacy checked.

He nodded morosely. "You'd think I'd said the

fop already had six wives, the way she turned on me." He shook his head.

Stacy noticed that his obvious agitation was attracting attention, and she playfully drew a circle with her finger on the sleeve of his coat. Looking up at him, she let her eyes flirt with him while she said, "I think we ought to find a more secluded spot to talk about this. You are being noticed."

He looked about him in surprise, and blushed slightly to see that he was the object of many people's attention. Laughing nervously, he looked down at Stacy. "How do I always manage to make a cake of myself?" She shook back her curls and laughed up at him. "Well, wise one," he said elaborately, "are you willing to give me the benefit of your sage counsel in this matter?"

"I should be happy to," she said, trying to achieve equal solemnity but failing.

Jeremy's face lightened as she laughed. "I think the conservatory would be suitably risqué, don't you?" Offering her his arm, he led her away, passing through several card rooms and by a well-laden buffet table, totally unaware of the black look that Anthony gave them as their laughing figures were lost from his sight.

"I don't know what has happened to her lately," Jeremy said sharply as he led her through the door of Lord Attenborough's small conservatory. It was filled with wildly growing plants, and the scent of exotic flowers filled the air with its intoxication. A winding path meandered among the plants, but Jeremy just stomped along it as if he were walking down the street. "She's changed," he added mournfully.

Stacy looked up from a flower that she was smelling. "I gather that you don't approve of the change," she said dryly. Another plant caught her eye, and she drifted down the path toward it.

"Of course I don't," he shouted after her. "She was fine the way she was. Everybody liked her." Stacy disappeared along the path and, muttering impatiently, he trailed along after her.

"You didn't," Stacy said calmly. She sat on a bench along the path, leaving enough room for him.

"That's ridiculous!" Jeremy snapped, sitting heavily next to her. "I did too like her."

Stacy could not keep from laughing, which only increased his scowl. "You have not appeared to care much about her," she teased, "until she found someone she likes better."

"But that's just it!" Jeremy cried triumphantly. "She can't prefer Sheridan. He's such a fool!"

"I think you're jealous," Stacy laughed, and stood up. "You thought she'd always be there when you wanted her, but now you are afraid you've lost her."

Jeremy stood up and walked a short distance away from her. "That's nonsense," he insisted quickly. "And I wasn't talking about myself. I'm concerned about this apparent fascination she has for Sheridan. I had hoped that you could talk some sense into her."

"Me?" Stacy asked with a laugh. She walked over to a rosebush and thoughtfully rubbed a blossom with her thumb. "I'd be the wrong one to talk to her, because I think she's doing the right thing."

"What!" Jeremy shrieked.

Stacy let go of the flower and turned to face him. It was dim in the room, but she could see the look of astonishment on his face. "I was very aware of her feelings for you," she said bluntly, "and thought she was a fool. You were constantly rude to her and ignored her, but her adoration never faltered. I don't know why it suddenly did, but I'm quite glad about it. It's about time she noticed that there are other men in the world beside you. It's quite obvious that you don't care a fig about her, so she ought to find someone who will."

Jeremy was clearly shocked by her words. "But Sheridan?" he protested weakly.

"Oh, I'm ready to admit he wouldn't be my choice, but anyone can see that he treats her far better than you ever did," Stacy said lightly.

"I might have known that you'd stick up for her," Jeremy muttered in disgust. "You don't know anything about the situation," he accused, then turned abruptly and stalked out of the conservatory.

Stacy sat down again and leaned back. She put her hand up and wearily rubbed her forehead. Perhaps it had been a mistake, saying all that to Jeremy, but she was so tired of this elaborate dance of manners in which no one ever bothered to speak the truth. Well, Jeremy had it now, and she could only hope that she hadn't spoiled Cecilia's chances completely.

She stood up to return to the drawing room, when she realized that someone was standing a few feet away from her.

"Are you all right?" Anthony asked. "I saw Jeremy come out by himself, and I was worried."

Stacy stood up and shook her hair back from her face, the movement giving her a small amount of confidence. "There was no reason to be worried," she laughed. "I was just making myself a little more presentable." She smoothed down imaginary wrinkles in her skirt and brushed off her small puffy sleeves. "I felt rather disheveled," she added teasingly.

Anthony did not move as Stacy had hoped he would, so she squared her shoulders, took a deep breath, and tried to slide past him. She thought she had made it, when a cold hand shot out and grabbed her arm. "Just what kind of a game are you playing now?" he asked coldly.

She tried to pull her arm away, but he held her firmly. "I don't know what you are talking about," she laughed, a quiver of nervousness in her voice, "but I really ought to get back to Lady Elinor."

His other hand reached out to hold her, so that she

223

couldn't even turn away. "I see," he snapped. "You can waste hours with that fool Chetwin, but you can't bear to spend a few minutes here with me."

Stacy shrugged. His nearness was affecting her, and she feared that if she had to speak she would only burst into tears.

"If you are trying to punish me for this morning, you are doing an excellent job," he grated.

"Oh, this morning!" she scoffed. "I hope you didn't take all that seriously. It was just a bit of fun."

Stacy looked up into his eyes, and shivered with fear at the black look of anger there. She tried again to free herself, but his grip only became tighter. "So you were lying when you said you loved me?" he whispered harshly.

She refused to answer, tossing her head angrily. "What difference does it make? It's not as if your feelings are involved."

He pulled her closer to him. "And they aren't?" he demanded.

Stacy squirmed uneasily. "If they were, you wouldn't be marrying your precious Blanche," she pointed out. "You must think I'm a fool to believe that!"

"My God!" he muttered under his breath. "You are driving me insane."

With a sudden movement he pulled her into his arms and began to kiss her ruthlessly. Stacy fought against him, knowing that all too quickly the ecstasy

224

of his kiss would melt all her resistance, making her love for him obvious. But her feeble struggles seemed to inflame him further, and his arms crushed her tighter and tighter to him.

Suddenly she was caught in the fire of his passion. She forgot her silly argument and her attempt to hide her love. His lips tormented and caressed her as he murmured words of love against her skin. She clung to him, hungering for his touch and trembling with longing for him.

Along with the unbelievable happiness she felt, a nagging fear rose. She kept pushing it away, refusing to think of anything that might spoil this perfect moment, but somehow it broke through, and silent tears coursed down her cheeks.

Anthony drew back slowly when he tasted the tears on her cheeks. Neither of them spoke for a moment, then he pulled her back into his arms and let her lie against his chest. The tears continued to flow, although she tried to stop them, but he didn't say a word. He just put his snowy white handkerchief into her hand.

Once she had finally stopped crying, she reluctantly left the comfort of his arms. She blotted her cheeks softly, hoping that her eyes were not puffy and red, while they walked slowly down the pathway.

"I'm sorry," Anthony said contritely. "I should not have come here."

She took the linen away from her eyes, but looked

straight ahead at a flower and not at him. "I take it that you have not changed your mind since this morning," she asked, trying to keep her voice steady.

Anthony shook his head silently, deciding that it would do no good to tell her of the scene with Blanche earlier. He took a step closer, but stopped when he saw her body stiffen. "You make it sound as simple as changing my coat," he argued, "but it's not. I gave my word, and there's nothing I can do now. It doesn't matter what I would prefer."

Stacy closed her eyes briefly, forbidding more tears to come. She was through crying over Anthony. She opened them again as he began to speak.

"I want you to know," he said quietly, "that I will always love you." She said nothing, so he went on. "I know you are upset now," he said "but you are young, and there will be someone else, someone who will mean as much to you as you do to me."

Stacy closed her eyes to the pain in his voice, and turned slowly around to face him. "Yes, you are right," she said with remarkable calm. "I know there will be someone else, and if you will excuse me, I think I would prefer being at the party where I might find him." She turned and walked regally out of the room.

CHAPTER FOURTEEN

Stacy dressed with meticulous care for Blanche's ball, as if a lovely appearance could shield her from the pain of Anthony's betrothal.

She sat very still as Mary arranged her curls and helped her into her dress. It was a lovely creation of white crepe with a pale pink underskirt, but Stacy did not notice it, or how beautiful she looked in the mirror she passed on her way down the stairs. She had carefully locked all of her feelings deep inside her, and she had vowed that nothing would break through the wall of cool composure she had worked so hard to erect.

Lady Elinor greeted her quietly, and once Laurie

came down, they all silently climbed into the carriage.

"I cannot believe that he means to marry that woman," Lady Elinor sighed as the carriage trundled through the streets.

Laurie looked at her in surprise. "Why not?" he asked. "He always said he was going to."

His grandmother looked over at Stacy, who was staring out the window. "I had thought at one time that he was very attracted to Stacy," she said.

Laurie let out a loud crack of laughter. "Anthony and Stacy!" he cried, shaking his head. "Why, Stacy wouldn't give a pence for him!"

Laurie continued to laugh quietly while Lady Elinor watched Stacy. She was still staring out the window and did not deny Laurie's words. The old lady sighed loudly.

"It looks like I'll have to invite that woman over for tea, after all," she muttered. "But maybe, . . . I could serve a little hemlock . . ."

Laurie laughed again. "Accept it, Grandmother. They are both happy with the situation. Anthony is getting just what he wants."

"Is he?" she asked doubtfully as the carriage pulled to a stop. She glanced over at Stacy, who seemed very pale. "Are you all right, child?" she asked in concern. "Perhaps we shouldn't have come."

"Why, I'm fine." Stacy forced herself to smile.

"And I'm quite happy to be here. I've looked forward to this ball for a long time."

Lady Elinor looked highly skeptical, but she said nothing as she was helped from the carriage. Stacy took advantage of the brief respite. She breathed in deeply and shook her head slightly. It was not going to be as easy as she thought to retain her fragile hold on her emotions.

Blanche was so busy attending to minor details when Anthony arrived for the ball that she allowed him to wander off by himself. He had the great fortune to find a footman pouring out glasses of champagne. After his second glass he felt able to face Blanche again, although it was with fatalistic resignation. He would do what he had to do, but his heart would always belong to Stacy. He turned back to the footman and helped himself to a third glass of champagne.

"Isn't this a wonderful ball?" Blanche enthused when he joined her near the door.

He nodded bleakly as Stacy, Laurie, and his grandmother came in. Stacy was even more beautiful than he had remembered.

Blanche and her mother greeted them enthusiastically. "I am so glad that you could come," Blanche cooed to Lady Elinor. "I have so looked forward to meeting you."

Lady Elinor nodded with the barest civility, and

turned to Anthony as some other guests were greeted.

"I cannot believe you are going through with
this," she hissed at him. "But it's not too late. There's
been no formal announcement. Tell her you've
changed your mind."

Anthony sighed and moved away from Blanche
and her mother. He looked sadly over at Stacy, but
she gave no sign of her feelings. "It really is too late,"
he told his grandmother gently. "I know you feel I'm
making a mistake, but you mustn't let yourself worry
about it. Just let me take care of my own life."

Stacy broke in with a stilted laugh. "It's not as if
he has been forced into this," she reminded Lady
Elinor. "He chose the woman he really cares about
for his wife, and is ready to make a life together with
her. It's a reason to be happy," she said, smiling
brightly, "and I for one intend to enjoy myself tonight."

She flashed a dazzling smile as Jeremy joined
them. Slipping her arm through his, she scolded
lightly, "I've been waiting for you. It was very
naughty of you to take so long." She quickly turned
him away from Anthony, so that Jeremy's look of
astonishment was hidden from the others.

So that was it, Anthony thought murderously,
watching them disappear. All that talk of love had
only been words, for Stacy was certainly suffering no
pangs of despair. And he had thought that she would

be suffering as he was! He laughed scornfully. What a fool he was!

A footman passed by with a tray of glasses, and Anthony took two of them. He drank one quickly, and put the empty glass down next to a potted palm behind him. The other he drained in one gulp as well, but held onto it, twisting it broodingly in his hands.

"What was that all about?" Jeremy whispered as he and Stacy moved away.

Stacy thought quickly. "I wanted to talk to you," she told him. "I . . . wanted to apologize for what I said to you yesterday."

Jeremy looked even more astonished. "But I wasn't really angry at you," he assured her. "I know you were right, now that I've had time to think about it. Cecilia is the one I really care about."

He looked so miserable that Stacy forgot her own problems. "Is Cecilia here tonight?" she asked.

He nodded. "With that Sheridan fellow again."

"Did you speak with her?"

"I asked her to save me a dance, but she wasn't sure she had any free," he said bitterly. "How can I ask her to marry me if she won't even dance with me?" he cried.

"Do you want me to speak to her?" Stacy asked reluctantly.

"Would you?" he agreed eagerly. "Just tell her how I feel about her."

Stacy held up one hand quickly. "No," she said. "I will try to convince her to give you another chance, but I am not going to relate messages between the two of you. You must summon up the courage to face her yourself."

Jeremy nodded, a worried look on his face. "I guess I can try," he said uncertainly.

Stacy's lips tightened in exasperation as she went back to Lady Elinor's side. She was just in time to see Blanche and Anthony begin the dancing together.

"They make a lovely couple," Stacy said stiffly, for some reason feeling forced to make a comment.

Lady Elinor gave her a black look. "He is a fool!" she said succinctly.

Stacy blinked back the tears burning in the corners of her eyes, and watched the couple on the floor. "When will they make the announcement?" she asked.

"Later in the evening," Lady Elinor said. Looking closely at Stacy, she offered, "We don't have to stay."

Stacy turned and saw Mr. Granger approaching her. "And miss all this fun?" She shook her head at Lady Elinor and allowed him to lead her onto the floor.

Stacy soon learned that the best way to fight her love for Anthony was to flirt outrageously with everyone else. Perhaps if she could convince Anthony that she did not really love him, then she might begin to believe it herself.

Aware that he was off to the side of the ballroom watching her, Stacy laughed her way through the dance with Mr. Granger and smiled through one with Sir Clifford. During her waltz with Jeremy, she teased and cajoled him until he was smiling too, his moodiness left far behind.

Anthony watched as Stacy danced with one gentleman after another. It was too much for him. Why should everyone else but he be able to enjoy her company? The one thing that he really wanted was to hold her in his arms, even if it would be for the last time; instead, he had to watch while strangers touched her. Filled with sudden resolution, he marched across the ballroom in search of her.

After their dance, Jeremy did not take Stacy back to Lady Elinor's side but led her over to Cecilia and Mrs. Frayne. He gave her hand a meaningful squeeze and went in search of a glass of lemonade for her.

"Jeremy has been very upset about you," Stacy said to Cecilia, who shrugged.

"I haven't noticed," she said coolly as her eyes flashed over the crowd. She smiled a greeting to an acquaintance across the floor.

Stacy watched her silently for a moment. "Cecilia," she said suddenly, "you aren't angry with me, are you?"

Cecilia turned to her in honest surprise. "With

you?" she exclaimed. "Of course not. Why would I be angry with you?"

Stacy smiled with relief. "I have been with Jeremy a bit, and you didn't seem happy to see me . . ."

Cecilia reached over and patted her hand. "It was your companion that I wasn't very pleased to see. I'm always happy to see you."

"Don't you think you are being a bit hard on him?" Stacy ventured.

"Not at all." Cecilia laughed.

People began to take their places on the floor for the next set, and Stacy saw Mr. Sheridan heading in their direction.

"But you aren't serious about Mr. Sheridan, are you?" she asked fearfully.

Cecilia laughed in real delight. "Now that had to be Jeremy," she said, shaking her head with a smile. "I find it hard to believe that you would even consider such a possibility." She laughed quietly to herself. "But after wasting so much time watching Jeremy, it's quite nice to have a gentleman be concerned about me, and I have been taking advantage of it."

"Just so long as you are in no danger of becoming the next Mrs. Sheridan," Stacy said quietly.

"Are you free for this dance?" a quiet voice asked Stacy.

She looked up to see Anthony standing in front of her. Her heart seemed to stop beating, but she refused to let him see any sign of it.

"No, I'm not," she said with a polite smile, seeing Mr. Sheridan coming up behind him. "Actually, here's my partner now." She greeted Mr. Sheridan with a bright smile, and took his arm. He was not accustomed to finding such eager partners, and led her away without a murmur of dissent.

Stacy kept her eyes laughingly with her partner and did not look back to see Anthony staring after her. She did see Jeremy walking toward Cecilia, though, so soon they might be working out their difficulties. It was a happy thought that was reflected in the sparkle in her eyes.

Cecilia also saw Jeremy coming, but was not prepared to welcome him. She hurried over to Anthony's side just as Jeremy reached her.

"Isn't this our dance?" she said loudly.

Anthony turned to look at her in surprise. He did not recall asking her to dance but obediently led her across the floor. He felt very dull-witted as they took their place in the set.

Stacy was unfortunately lost in her thoughts and unaware of Cecilia's actions. It was quite a shock for her, then, when her eyes met Jeremy's across the floor and his were very definitely scowling at her. She looked about at the couples in confusion and saw Cecilia. She was dancing with Anthony!

Stacy knew that Cecilia and Anthony were nothing more than friends, but the sight of them dancing together was more than she could bear. She felt ready to burst into tears. No amount of self-scolding made the slightest difference. She could not stay at the ball. If she couldn't bear to watch him dancing with her friend, how could she ever stand here and congratulate him on his engagement to Blanche?

When the music stopped, Mr. Sheridan was ready to lead Stacy out into the garden so that she might better appreciate his many talents, but she had other ideas and hurried over to Lady Elinor's side.

"Do you think we could leave?" she asked her plaintively.

The old lady was understanding. "Of course," she agreed. "I've no desire to stay either."

"But Miss Prescott," Mr. Sheridan wailed, "I've only had one dance with you."

Stacy turned to him in surprise, not even aware that he had followed her off the dance floor. "I'm sorry," she apologized uncertainly. Her hand rubbed her forehead in agitation. "But I have a terrible headache . . ."

"I understand." He was all consideration. "Perhaps, instead, I might call on you tomorrow."

"If you like." Stacy was barely listening. Anthony had seen them standing and was coming toward them, a puzzled look on his face.

"Stacy," a scolding voice called from behind her. "I thought you said you would speak to her."

She turned with a sigh. "I did, Jeremy," she assured him, "but I never promised that I would be able to change her mind."

"She hates me even more now," he complained. "What did you say to her?"

Lady Elinor took Stacy's arm. "Are you ready now?" she asked her quietly.

Stacy nodded, and the two of them tried to thread their way through the crowd.

"Stacy!" Jeremy called after her, but she kept on going, an unreasoning terror growing in her that she mustn't let Anthony catch up with them.

A firm grip on her arm pulled her to an abrupt stop. She spun around to see Anthony looking down at her.

"Where are you going?" he asked quietly, such a look of bewildered pain in his eyes that Stacy had to look away.

"We are going home," Lady Elinor replied, saving Stacy from having to answer him.

His fingers loosened their grip on her arm but stayed in their place, gently caressing. "Can't you stay for just one dance?" he begged her.

Stacy looked up for a moment, but her eyes filled with tears and she turned away. What heaven it would be to dance with him one more time! To pretend for a short time that they would always be together and that there wasn't someone else to claim him once they left the floor! What sweet madness!

"No," she said softly, shaking her head. Turning away toward the entrance, she said, "We can't stay."

He dropped his hand, and the place on her arm felt suddenly cold. Unconsciously she rubbed the spot while Lady Elinor steered her toward the door.

"But you can't be leaving already," Blanche said, hurrying up to them as they waited for Laurie. "We haven't made our announcement yet." She slid her arm through Anthony's and smiled up at him possessively.

"The evening has been too much for me," Lady Elinor said weakly with a pathetic cough. "I rarely go out in society, you know."

Blanche nodded sympathetically while Stacy turned to Laurie, who had just hurried up. "Are you ready?" she asked quietly.

Lady Elinor nodded to Blanche and started to turn away. Suddenly she stopped and turned to face her. "You must come to tea one day next week," she invited, with only the barest hint of warmth in her voice.

"I would be honored to," Blanche said quickly, her eyes glowing with excitement. "Would Thursday be convenient?"

Lady Elinor shrugged, then nodded her head. "That would be fine," she agreed stiffly.

Knowing what an effort it was for her to issue that invitation, Stacy took Lady Elinor's arm and squeezed her hand. Laurie went ahead to the carriage while Stacy helped the old woman down the hall.

At the door she turned back, knowing that Anthony was still there, and their eyes met. Blanche was clinging to his arm, talking earnestly to him, but she was unaware of his distraction. Stacy looked at him, her eyes full of her love, and saw in his the agony he was suffering. She smiled sadly, then went out the door.

CHAPTER FIFTEEN

Blanche was still chattering away as the door closed behind Stacy, but Anthony shook her hand off his arm and despondently walked back into the ballroom. He pushed his way past the other guests and walked to a small table in the corner.

He helped himself to two quick glasses of champagne, then turned away in disgust, fingering a third glass. All the wine he had consumed should have dulled some of the pain he was feeling, but it hadn't. Neither had it drowned the rage that burned within him when he saw Stacy even look at another man.

He walked slowly away from the crowds of people, thoughtfully twisting his glass in his hand. After tonight things would move rapidly. Within a few weeks the season would be over, and he and Blanche would be married. They would settle into his country home, but he had no idea where Stacy would be. Married herself, most likely, since that was the purpose of her stay in the city.

Anthony found himself on the terrace and stared out into the darkness of the garden. He could see Stacy laughing and smiling at all the men she had danced with this evening. Would she choose one of them to marry? The thought of his lovely Stacy in the arms of another man tore at him. He could feel her sweet lips beneath his, and knew that sometime soon another would taste her sweetness. Someone else's hands would touch her, and she would cling to that man as she had once clung to him.

Suddenly the rage broke through. He turned and threw his glass against the wall of the house, where it shattered in a spray of champagne. The couples around him edged away, silently watching his next move.

"I've felt like that myself," a light voice laughed at his side.

Anthony turned and saw Jeremy smiling at him. He was carrying two full glasses of champagne. "Would you like a replacement?" he offered.

Anthony nodded in embarrassment and took one of the glasses. "I, uh . . . . don't quite know what came over me," he said hesitantly.

Jeremy shrugged his shoulders. "Excitement over

your upcoming nuptials, perhaps?" he guessed. Taking a long drink from his glass, Jeremy turned to lean his arms on the railing that ran along the edge of the terrace. He looked out into the darkness. "I've decided that Blanche is right," he said simply. "It's time that I stopped playing games and settled down." He sighed, thinking of how his indecisiveness had lost Cecilia to him forever. Well, he would marry Stacy instead. He did not love her, but they could be reasonably happy. "I'm afraid that I had to learn my lesson the painful way," he said bitterly.

Anthony had finished off his drink and was attempting to balance the glass on the top of the railing. "Oh?" he said politely.

"If you'll be home tomorrow, I thought we might discuss the settlement and such things."

Anthony became very still. His head turned slowly until he was facing Jeremy. "Why would you come to me about settlements?" His voice was deathly quiet.

Jeremy slightly laughed. "I assumed that you were Stacy's guardian," he said, "but apparently you aren't." He shook his head, still looking at the garden. "Whom do I see? Do you know?"

Anthony stared at him, making no effort to control the anger surging through him. "Stacy!" he whispered harshly. "Stacy!" His voice became louder, and Jeremy turned to look at him in astonishment. "How can you stand there and talk to me about marrying Stacy? Have you no feelings?" His voice was attracting attention.

Jeremy shook his head helplessly and spread his hands in appeal. "I thought you were her guardian," he said, not sure why Anthony was so upset.

But Anthony was beyond reasoning. He had been building up a violent hatred for the man Stacy would eventually wed, and now he suddenly found that very man right in front of him. "You can't have her!" he cried, and, his hands outstretched, he lunged at Jeremy.

The wine Anthony had consumed had addled his thinking and slowed his reflexes, but all he could think about was striking out at the man who would have Stacy. He did not notice the chair that was between them or the fact that Jeremy had jumped back in surprise. He grabbed wildly, meaning to choke the life out of him, only to find himself falling amid table- and chair-legs. Lying back in his undignified position, he glared up at Jeremy, who was trying to hide a smile.

Suddenly someone flew out of the crowd and threw herself into Jeremy's arms. "Oh, Jeremy, are you hurt?" Cecilia cried in concern. She turned quickly to give Anthony a black look. "How dare you try to hurt Jeremy, you horrible, horrible man!" she said to him in disgust. Her voice was all concern, though, as she turned back to Jeremy and fussed over him. "Are you hurt badly?"

Jeremy winked over her shoulder at Anthony, and moaned slightly. "I think I will be all right," he gasped weakly.

Cecilia was horrified. "You must sit down," she exclaimed. "No, lie down. We'll send for a doctor."

"No," Jeremy said wickedly, pushing her away. "You must go back to Mr. Sheridan. I daresay I can manage on my own." He closed his eyes and moaned again.

"I'm not going anywhere," she insisted, putting his arm around her shoulders. "Here, you can lean on me, and we'll go somewhere quiet where you can rest." Leaning heavily on her, he limped a few feet away. He looked back over his shoulder at Anthony. "Thanks, old man," he mouthed with a wink, then turned back to Cecilia with a pitiful moan.

Anthony watched them leave the terrace, feeling like a fool. Leaning heavily on one hand, he began to rise from the debris, only to stop when he noticed an impatiently tapping foot next to his hand. He looked up to see Blanche glaring down at him.

"Oh, is it time to make the announcement already?" he asked.

Lady Elinor pulled her shawl closer around her and settled back in her chair, staring into the shadows of her bedroom. She was getting too old for all this emotional nonsense, she decided cynically. She looked up, irritated by a disturbance out in the street.

She ought to move to the country, she thought, and hire a musty old companion. If she refused to see anyone, especially relations, she might have a chance to enjoy what was left of her life.

The commotion outside was getting louder rather than dying down, so she rose impatiently to send a footman outside to chase the noisemakers away. She walked across the floor and threw open her door, only to discover that the shouting seemed even louder.

Curiously she walked along the hallway to the top of the stairs. James, the footman, was having difficulty with someone at the door.

"Who is it, James?" she called angrily.

James turned at the sound of her voice, carefully closing the door first. "It's Lord Kendall, my lady," he told her.

"Anthony?" she asked in surprise. "Is he foxed?" As she came down a few steps, a pounding was heard at the door and something unintelligible was shouted.

James fastidiously wrinkled his nose. "It appears so," he said.

More shouting and pounding were heard. "For God's sake, send him home," Lady Elinor said in disgust, and turned to go back upstairs.

Unfortunately, just as the footman opened the door slightly to relay the message, Anthony threw his full weight against it. The door swung open,

James fell backward, and Anthony staggered in. He regained his balance quickly and brushed off his clothes. Although it made little difference to all his wrinkles and stains, he seemed satisfied.

Noticing that James was preparing to throw him bodily out the door, he moved to the side of the hall. "Stacy!" he shouted out. "Stacy!"

Lady Elinor came back down the steps. "Go home and get some sleep," she scolded him not unkindly.

He eyed James advancing toward him and called out again. "Stacy!"

"Anthony!" his grandmother said more severely. "You can't see the poor child now. She's asleep already. Come back tomorrow."

James held open the door. "If you please, my lord," he said stiffly.

Anthony moved to the bottom of the staircase and looked up pleadingly at his grandmother. "Can't I see her for just a moment?"

"In this disgusting condition?" Lady Elinor shook her head. "If you are alive in the morning, come back then."

A movement above them caused them all to look up to the top of the stairs. Stacy had come to see what was happening. She had hastily pulled a pink dressing gown around her nightgown, and small wisps of lace were visible at the neck. Her eyes were swollen and red, testifying as to how she had spent the last hour.

"Stacy!" Anthony cried happily. He started up the stairs, only to find his way blocked by his grandmother.

"Anthony, what's wrong?" Stacy asked, wearily pushing the curls back from her face.

"Nothing!" he cried with an infectious grin. He threw his arms open wide. "I'm free!" he shouted.

Laurie joined Stacy at the top of the stairs, but she didn't notice him. "What do you mean?" she whispered, then looked at his wrinkled and stained clothing. "What has happened to you?"

"I tried to kill Jeremy, and Blanche threw me out," he said proudly.

"You tried to kill someone?" His grandmother was horrified, but Anthony had forgotten she was there.

"She threw you out of the ball?" Stacy asked fearfully.

Anthony shook his head with a laugh. "No, she threw me out forever!" he said.

"Anthony, was he hurt?" Lady Elinor persisted worriedly.

Anthony ignored her as he smiled at Stacy. "She said she was badly mistaken in my character, and I told her that Star was a stupid name for a horse." He laughed, then frowned up the stairs at her. "You are too far away," he complained. "Will you come down, or shall I come up?"

Lady Elinor suddenly came to her senses. "You

will go home," she ordered sternly. "I don't care what has happened tonight. It's no excuse for your disgusting appearance." She became aware that he was paying no attention to her but watching something just beyond her. She turned quickly as Stacy slipped behind her. "Stacy! Go back to your room!" she ordered. "You aren't dressed!"

Stacy walked down the last few steps slowly, her eyes solemnly on Anthony, and stopped just before the bottom. He came over and took her hands in his, looking adoringly up at her.

"Will you marry me, Stacy?" he asked simply.

She nodded quickly, an excited smile spreading over her face. "Oh, yes, yes," she cried, and threw her arms around his neck.

Anthony's arms gently enfolded her as his head bent down, his lips seeking hers. When they touched, it was with such blinding ecstasy that both he and Stacy forgot their audience and lost themselves in the world of their love.

Lady Elinor looked down at them with a smile, having abandoned her attempts to send Anthony home. This was what she had wanted all along, she reminded herself, so what did it matter if their behavior was slightly improper?

Love—the way you want it!

Candlelight Romances

THE DARK HORSEMAN

Marianne Harvey

author of *The Proud Hunter*

Beautiful Donna Penroze had sworn to her
dying father that she would save her sole leg-
acy, the crumbling tin mines and the ancient,
desolate estate *Trencobban*. But the mines
were failing, and Donna had no one to turn to.
No one except the mysterious Nicholas Tre-
varvas—rich, arrogant, commanding. Donna
would do anything but surrender her pride, anything but admit her irresistible longing for *The
Dark Horseman.*

A Dell Book $3.25

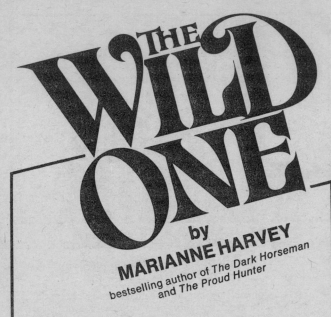

THE WILD ONE

by
MARIANNE HARVEY
bestselling author of *The Dark Horseman*
and *The Proud Hunter*

Proud, beautiful Judith—raised by her stern
grandmother on the savage Cornish coast—
boldly abandoned herself to one man and sought
solace in the arms of another. But only one man
could tame her, could match her fiery spirit,
could fulfill the passionate promise of rapturous,
timeless love.

A Dell Book $2.95   (19207-2)

Dell Bestsellers